My Last First Kiss

From the
Baptized N' Warm Milk Collection
Based on
Temptations of the Flesh

by
DeVondia R. Roseborough

My Last First Kiss
By DeVondia R. Roseborough

ISBN 978-0-615-46667-5

Written & Published by: DeVondia R. Roseborough
Cover Design by: Moye'
Formatting: Marcus Kiser
Edited by Candy Green
Wardrobe: Passion
Make-up: Ebony Mobley-Henderson
Hair: MasterKutz Stylist

Printed in the United States of America

Other books by
DeVondia R. Roseborough

PUT IT ON PAPER

Contents

For my cousin…
James Pratt Hood, Jr.:

Waheed, I didn't get the opportunity to
have my book in your bookstore, cousin,
but you got your name in my book.
I love you and miss you…
ASHE

Acknowledgements

For my Father God, my Daddy...This book has everything to do with what I and I alone, allowed to happen, but You, Father God, brought me through and You get all the Glory.

First, I have to say "Thank You, Lord," for all You have done in my life. I really appreciate the changes you are making within me.

I once told You, "You can trust me," and You have granted my every wish, performed every miracle and made the desires of my heart into Your Promises kept.

I know I have a crazy faith in You and You only. I always try to praise You in advance. You have shown me so many times when I thought this book was ready to be released that You had some more flesh to peel off before it could reach the masses.

My words were pulled apart as the role You played in all of these things was brought forth.

The book cover was recreated to fit the lessons I am learning: You and You alone are the Author and Finisher of my Faith...and this book.

I thank You, Lord, for delivering me from toxic people places and things, for getting them out of my way, life and spirit—with little help from me at times. For these interventions, I thank You, Daddy, for loving me as You do.

To my beautiful daughters, Camisha and Shyla... You two have grown into such lovely ladies and make me proud to call you mine. Continue to keep God first, pray before the test, during the storm and when the wind subsides. I love you forever and always.

To my beautiful Mama... You are the best mother in the whole wide world. You have been my shoulder through buckets of tears and my backup in every sticky situation. I thank God for you being who you are to me and my girls. You mean so much to me and I love you unconditionally.

Hey, Joe Blow... Smile...You have never been a "step-daddy." You have been a father to me and the best grandfather of them all. Thanks for keeping your promise to my grandmother to take care of her daughter and her girls. You are a respectful man of honor. I love you for all you have done to keep our family together. Through all the tough times you held on. May God bless you for being present—you are a gift.

My dear little sister, LaTeka Roseborough... We don't talk too much or get along as we should, but I love you from afar. I am proud of you for making the Dean's List. Keep pushing, Baby Oprah!

To my brothers, Terry and Michael... Thanks for taking the time out to get to know me and spend time with your little sister. I love you guys.

To my favorite cousin, Robert Burris... You have brought the Cadillac back to life so many times. I appreciate you "keeping me on the road."

To the most creative book cover designer and amazing photographer this side of Heaven...Moye, you are the truth. It has been a pleasure working with you over the years and look forward to many more. Continue to "harness your Super Powers." **To my Editor...Candy Green**, it has been a pleasure working with you. You have taught me so much about making my written words available to all--not just to those who know me, but to others my stories can touch. Thank you for taking the time to break things down for me, for the things I didn't know, and for accepting my tough skin when I didn't back down. You are a "ram in the bush."

To Founder and Great Late Bishop C.M. Beatty, Jr... You said to me, "Sister Roseborough, what is your next book going to be about?" I gave you the title and you rubbed your head and said, "That's going to make a lot of money." Thank you, Bishop Beatty, for being my leader and father in the Gospel. You instilled a lot of wisdom and I carry it wherever I go in my heart. **First Lady Bishop and Chemaria (Beatty Baby)**—I love you!

To my cousin and makeup artist, Ebony Mobley-Henderson, and you, too, Shrek...LOL (Taras)...I told you they were coming out with Part Three! I love you guys—you, too, **Courtney and Darius**.

To my cousin, Candy Walker...and my little cousin, Shaquanda Walker, too!

To Antonio (Monkey) Rogers, my other brother from another mother...I love you and am glad to have you back home. Keep pushing the right way.

To my best friends in the whole wide world...you ladies are definitely true to the words *loyalty* and *friendship*. Bump what you heard. These are Black Girls who ROCK! Angela Bush...girl, we have been doing this since '87...LOL; Tiffany Barringer...my Ace, my Bestie, the one who plays no games; Pam Lanier...I am glad you are back in my life, lady. Thanks for the awesome conversations over croaker and grits; Natasha Fetterson...I love you because you are my Sunshine; Veronica Crawford...my sister from another who has a laugh and the famous walk we call The Wiggler; Michelle Brooks...my sister in Christ (Lenny)...never heard nothing twice... thanks for listening and advising in a godly way; my MasterKutz Crew: Slow, Big Game, Fame, Jr., Ms. Doris, Sovanny...thanks for doing my lashes.

My author friends...Cornelia Gail, Marcus Massy, Charmean Gregory, Cheryl Mayfield...you DIVA; Artellia Burch...thanks for the blurb; Andrea Blackstone: Thank you all for being an inspiration to me; Cheris Hodges...you have helped me in so many ways, lady. Thank you for everything you have done to assist me on this writer's journey.

Radio personality and heartthrob Ms. CC Mitchell...the Lady with the Voice: Thanks for shouting it out with me via text, via video, over the radio and on the back of my book—you are the bomb!

Ms. Coretta Livingston...I truly am grateful for the opportunities you have given me to voice my projects on your show: WGIV 103.3 FM The QC Broker Show. Thank you, also, to Nala Ruiz (WUFO Internet Radio)...Thank you for purchasing your first copy of the book last year. Talk about pre-sale! You are a "jewel lady." I love you for all you have done for me over the years. Thanks Fly Ty On-Air with My 92.7 FM...for your encouraging posts and witty delivery. Your support has meant a lot. My girl, Kim Williams...we have been down since the nickel on the needle. R. Kelly ROCKS!!! Love you, girl...

I cannot shout out everyone on **Facebook**, but I will get this here out of me!

Marcell Mazz Jackson...I have been loving you since fifth grade—you know what it is; **Netta "Betta" Jackson-Adams**... thanks for the encouraging words; **Teresa Legrand**...you are a piece of work, Woman of God. Continue to bless those with the Word of God; **Dorothy Woods**...I love you, lady—you post at the right time! **Trisha Huntley-Anderson (Pravis)**...you are a woman of change, lady—I admire you a lot. I remember when you hit me with your car and I tore your side mirror off. Look at us now. Bless you, lady; **Mother Rayon**...if only they knew the wisdom you possess. **To my church family at New Covenant Bibleway Church**...I love you all, but I must give honor to my "toe jam" of a friend, **Sherondie Coleman (Will)**...you keep the toes so fancy. **Mia Sloan-Conner, Veronica McKennith, Phanarve Beatty, Kami Beatty-Loadholt, Tovonia Hunter, Michelle Hinton (Mark), Tracy McCain, Gina McCain, Dashawn (Pop) Pratt.**

New Covenant Praise and Worship Team: continue to usher in the Lord. That's what it's all about: magnifying and glorifying through worship and song in truth. I love you guys.

To everyone else I didn't name: I love you—there's just too many of you! I will pencil you in on the next one—many more releases to come.

To my readers...I thank you all so much for hounding me on the release of my book, especially **Kawana Beatty**...it's finally here. Hey, **Tamika Robinson**...you didn't see your name when I asked you to read the Acknowledgements—I love you, girl. I appreciate each of you for supporting my books, **The Rasberrirose Foundation**, and I can't forget my fish fry's. Croaker up! You are all truly special to me and I love you for your continued support.

For my Pastor, C.M Beatty III, and First Lady, Dorothy Beatty...I close with a special note for you both. You two are a fresh start to a new beginning for this appointed time in my life. Thank you, both, for being true to the Word and sharing your testimony, Pastor. Thank you for allowing others to see that God did it for you, He can do it for me. Your father, my Bishop, couldn't have appointed a better person to influence me as you do. **First Lady,** you are a headstrong

Woman of God and I appreciate you acknowledging me one as well. I have been called many things, but it's nothing like being called a "blessed Woman of God." Thank you for depositing greatness in me. I love you guys more than words can say. I am blessed to be under your leadership. Thanks for being who you are.

God bless you all!
DeVondia Roseborough
2011

$\mathcal{P}rologue$

Seated for lunch at the University area Quiznos Sub Shop in my hometown of Charlotte, North Carolina, a friend asked me, "DeVondia, what is your second book going to be?"

"My Last First Kiss," I told her. "It's based on *Temptations of the Flesh*, for my collection **Baptized N' Warm Milk.** I want to reach the ones that are straddling the fence, not the half-hearted saints. I want to reach the ones who want to be wholehearted Christians."

She looked at me as if she was about to shout. She lifted her hand to give me a hi-five and said something that has never left my mind or heart. *"Whatever you write, DeVondia, please don't sugarcoat the issues that hinder our relationship with God. Keep it real, as you do best."*

This was a profound moment for me.

Ablavi Gbenyon, I thank you for sharing and encouraging the direction of this book.

I have struggled with the right words to use without being disrespectful to my readers. I found it was important to keep it real, as Ablavi asked.

People are of the flesh, so a lot of things people do or say don't surprise me anymore. People don't fear GOD or His powers. I, too, have been guilty of not being obedient.

What gets me is when we expect church people to act a certain kind of way and hold them high on a pedestal instead of accountable for their actions and sayings.

Believe it or not some church folk curse! Yes, they do.

Do not act like you haven't heard a slip of the tongue in the sanctuary or the fellowship hall because Sister Such-and-Such is pissed because all the macaroni was gone from last Sunday's dinner after church.

Some church folk fall weak to temptation:

Deacons drink liquor with their Deaconess wives after Bible Study...or smoke joints before turning the comforter back at a local hotel with their mistresses.

Who warms the pew on the right side of the church and squeezes her legs as the pastor stands to pray over the offertory plate?

Whatever you're doing, whoever you're doing it with, and what you're doing to satisfy the selfish needs of the flesh, you are doing while thinking you are hiding it from everybody.

God has His eyes on you at all times. Wherever you are in your faith, God waits for you to come to Him, regardless of what you have done.

God never leaves us. We are the ones who leave Him for a pleasure that lasts a minute--and has us wishing we had not later on.

Temptations of the Flesh...
Followed by Conviction!

As I searched how to put my thoughts on paper, I decided to use my personal journey to getting right with God as an outlet for letting go of the baggage that has plagued my flesh.

As I began writing, I noticed the men in my tale of flesh-gripping temptations carried more baggage than I did!

Then, more importantly, the Voice that spoke to me in late December 2008, had said, *"Use your experiences to help others."*

In His presence, those words were amplified through the hollow spaces in my mind. All that had occupied my thoughts was quickly removed by His presence and those words: *"Use your experiences to help others."*

Excited about this revelation from God, I said to Him, "Lord, I do not doubt You."

I giggled like Dora the Explorer with a fresh idea on her mind. "Lord, I need You to make it clear what it is You want me to do."

Just so I was sure it was God, I asked Him again to repeat Himself. I turned off the TV so I wouldn't be confused by anything or anyone. I felt a jerk in my neck as if someone had thumped me in the back of the head. I heard it loud and clear.

"Baptized N' Warm Milk, the Collection," He said. *"**My Last First Kiss** will be the first of a series of books to encourage women, with or without HIV--those who face the same temptations of the flesh you have."*

I cried like a baby while thanking Him in advance as I sought forgiveness for doubting His word. I had heard His voice, which really was a voiceless directive, to make a difference in the lives of others through my personal testimony. I should not be ashamed of what I have gone through, all the stress, as well as the mercy and grace that has gotten me to the other side.

In others words, I was to acknowledge where my help came from and who got me through the messes that, for the majority of the time, I had gotten myself into. God had finally given me another assignment and I was eager to get started.

As you are about to read, while going through my "go through," I got down, depressed, cried like a baby and shopped like crazy to ease the pain. These actions were a comforting coping mechanism I was accustomed to: I didn't want to think about the craziness that plagued my world.

I knew that once the crying stopped, the receipts from the shopping sprees would bring back the initial reason for the tears! But, after the tears, the depression would subside and the matters of the flesh would still need to be handled. So I started asking myself questions: How long would I dwell with these tears, in this depression? What was I going to do about it?

Music is and has always been a form of therapy for me. With sounds of The Love Zone on V-101.9 FM and DJ Preston "Mello"

Miles playing *On the Ocean*, my favorite song by K-Jon, I began to put my story on paper. With scented candles and a relaxed atmosphere to stimulate my creative juices…with soft lighting and good music to set the tone, my finger tips began to click on the Toshiba draining the pain that screamed in bold letters: **HELP!**

Once again, I hoped to encourage women everywhere to trust God first, set higher standards and expect a greater outcome--all the while patiently waiting their turn…

One

Well, it wouldn't be polite if I didn't honor the manners that were taught to me as a child.

Hello! Let me introduce myself. I'm Regina BoRose. I am a lovely, voluptuous sister who has accomplished much in her life and strives for the smell of extra success. Allow me to elaborate on "extra success."

Extra success means the more I give, the more people in need have. I dreamt a dream to do for others even when others don't reciprocate.

My heart is a queen—pure and golden--ruling over any princess, any day.

My skin is dark and smooth like butter. My lips are full with much to say between them. I have dreamy eyes that can discern the evilness of all and a smile that lights up any darkened soul. For all of that, I owe my Daddy, the Most High, for blessing me with these gifts and talents to encourage and inspire.

I stand about 5'9", weighing 190 pounds. Yeah, I don't mind telling my weight, age or height. I am a child of God and everything

He makes is good. As the Bible says, "You be ashamed of me, I will be ashamed of you." I am not ashamed of my God and I am confident in the skin I'm in today, as well as the age He's allowed me to see birthday after birthday. Even with a few extra pounds, I love me because I am in Him.

Yesterday was another story. The past is what it is...

I serve as a news contributor and, when it comes to Social Justice, writing for major magazines and newspapers is my passion. I have plenty to say; sometimes people care and sometimes they don't. My role is to set the record straight on issues that plague our society, especially in the Black community.

Health care for all, which includes those diagnosed with HIV/AIDS, is ravishing the community like popcorn in fresh grease. The dropout rate, teenage pregnancy and self-esteem are major issues among women and girls of color. Things need changing around these parts and I have opted to take on the challenge.

But, I didn't have much time to spend with a special someone. I was in a situation that was neither good nor healthy for me and I broke away after many attempts to break free as you will read. I'm not materialistic at all, so my problems weren't about having my nice house and nice cars. I share what I have with everyone who's close to me and has meaning in my life.

I have the greatest friends in the world.

Tiny is my stylist, short and dark-skinned, "thick to death," the guys at the shop call her. This sister has a beautiful face and her own fierce haircut. Tiny listens when I need to be heard and provides sound advice. She's married with children and loves the Lord. She has been doing my hair for over 15 years and I can see no one else ever slapping relaxer, cutting, shampooing or conditioning my black short crop. I dare not let it get out of hand.

Holiday is my girl from way back. She's a honey-brown diva who doesn't know whether she wants to be married or single--either way she "gets it in," as she calls it. She stands a mere 5'6" and has a body "like whoa," keeps a short haircut to match the big butt she bounces as she sashays through a crowd. Ms. Thing has the prettiest legs walking the earth. Holiday became a Grandma before any of us and enjoys family events at her house.

Sky is my road dog. Anytime I need a laugh and a way out of a pesky situation I call my girl Sky. She's 6'2" with hair cut short. Sky's as loud as any train or plane taking off. She was my "go to girl" when things got out of hand back in the day at the club.

Trina is my girl who has more in common with me than I would like. She has a very unique look about her. We Carolina girls are built Ford tough. Trina had a look that I was not used to seeing. She is beautiful, long legs and arms, with shiny black hair. She wears a lot of makeup, but it's not the kind that looks plastered on. She has a soft voice with a diamond-glow in her eye every time she smiles. But she had a secret that would make my world spin faster than bald tires on a fresh-rained street.

Jade is a workaholic who I only see during the holidays. She's 5'6" with honey-brown skin and a passion for bebe apparel. She's also quiet, but when it's time to speak she expresses herself as she pleases.

My friends are why I love my big house and many cars--so that we can get together and party, praise and catch up. Having all of this is a blessing, but not having someone special to share it with has been a challenge at times.

I love my friends, but they all have men or husbands in their lives. And this provoked my only burning question for God: "*When is it going to be my turn?*"

After six years of working with my organization, I was finally beginning to see fruits of my labor. I often spoke out on issues geared toward empowering African-American women with HIV, but I was not getting any major speaking roles.

Yeah, I was speaking out on issues that are dear to my heart and HIV is one of them, but in my striving to achieve, I got caught up with a man who promised we were inseparable. He had other things on his mind and out his pants.

I started searching my soul, praying for a way out of the mess I had gotten myself into. I have to admit, sometimes we don't fully let go of the past. It takes Someone Special to bring the best (and the worst) out of a no-win situation: I confessed it all to my Lord.

Now, I know, by God's grace, I will never step out of my element again seeking a love that was not meant to be. Being disobedient caused me to deny my promises to God.

But, God has never denied His promises to me.

My actions just prolonged the fruition.

Temptations of the Flesh...

Deep inside, I had a hidden part of me not seen by the naked eye nor felt by the human touch. This side wanted love and attention from the opposite sex. That side is…Me!

This was the same Me that had finally let go of her past but, at the same time, badly wanted a promising future in public speaking and motivational seminars.

I was tired of hearing my mom say she wanted to see at least one of her daughters marry before she died. I wanted badly to bring her wish to reality, but something was missing: a husband.

"You need some comfort and substance in your life," she was constantly saying. "You need someone that is going to love you in spite of your flaws and cherish all the love you have to give."

I listened to that same line over and over until it eventually sank in. She was right. It was time for me to stop doing the choosing and be chosen for a change.

I couldn't deal with the lonely part. It drained me.

I joined a church, not to look for love, but to seek a deeper relationship with God. However, to be blunt, all who desired my juices were married!

It turned out the produce section of the grocery store was not a hot spot for picking up a knight-in-shining-armor either...

That time I was sitting in the car at a local grocery waiting for my Godson's mom, Tee, to come out with his birthday cake. Instead, Tee was rushing every aisle for things she had forgotten: hotdogs, buns, ketchup, plates, etc.

Meanwhile, outside in my Range Rover, in 100 degree temperatures, I suddenly felt dizzy and nauseous. I decided to put my truck as close to the door as possible for immediate escape.

"Excuse me Miss, you can't park there," a security guard soon said. "This is the emergency lane."

"This is an emergency," I said. "I am near heat exhaustion—if not heat stroke. It's hitting me dead-smack in the face."

As I explained my brush with death and it being an emergency, I offered him my keys to move the car.

He agreed, and I slowly walked into the store.

I sat in the nearest seat available, securing me from meeting the floor face first. A red motorized grocery cart was my safety net.

A bottle of water from God-knows-whom helped replenish all that was drained from me--especially energy. My eyelashes were popping when I left the house, but was barely holding on to the natural extensions I was born with.

As I had recently lost twenty pounds in thirty days, I was excited about my new waistline. Just that morning I had picked up a nicely fitting pair of denim capris and a lime green T-top from Forever 21 in a neighboring mall. The denims fit my Size 14 body perfectly. The T-top accentuated my bust line and made everyone look--including women, who complimented on my new look.

My hair was spiked to perfection with tapered sides that lay down as if pasted on. "Lips shining as if chicken was about to be deep-fried," my cousin says to me all the time.

As I was sitting on the motorized grocery cart, a nice looking brown-skinned man walked past me and did a double take. I tried not to pay him any attention, being in my current condition and all.

However, his interest became noticeable due to his sudden bump into a produce sign that displayed, "Today's Sales & Specials."

Soon the security officer handed me my keys.

I continued to drink the water when a nice young boy around twelve or so gave me a Gatorade.

"Here you are Miss, this will help you out. It does wonders for me on the football field."

I smiled. "Thank you."

"No problem," he said. "I hope you feel better."

I looked down to make sure my right eyelash was still intact--at least until I got home.

Despite my near death experience, I was more concerned about how I looked in the overcrowded, understaffed grocery store. When I looked up, I was staring dead into the eyes of the man who had bumped into the sign.

He was standing near the floral section and to his right was a large vase with long-stemmed red roses. For many, apples keep the doctor away, but, for that moment, it was the red roses that brought me back to life. What a beautiful sight they were.

The strange man moved towards me with his left hand behind his back and presented me with a long-stemmed red rose.

"A pretty flower for a beautiful lady" he said with a smile that bought joy to my medically-alerted heart.

"Wow! Thanks," I said as I sniffed the essence of the flower. "Sorry, I didn't get your name."

"I'm Barry," he said. "I was intrigued by your beauty and couldn't start my shopping until I got the opportunity to hear your voice."

"I guess you must say that to all the ladies who almost pass out sitting in a hot Range Rover with the air turned off," I said with a half smile.

"No, pretty lady, I truly think you are a unique masterpiece. Your eyes are saying much more than your lips about wanting to share with a unique man like myself."

I gave him a seductive smile and batted my good eye--I have perfected the game, so do not try it at home.

"I'm Regina," I said, extending my arm to shake his hand with the ounce of strength the Gatorade had given me, quenching my body with energy.

"Thank you for the beautiful rose, Barry, and it's a pleasure to---"

"Regina," I heard Tee calling to me from a near-by check out. "I'm coming. I forgot a few things."

"Girl, I almost died out there in the heat waiting on you," I called back, "and all you had to get is his cake."

I watched the conveyor belt maneuver multiple items: beans, chips, sodas and whatever else-- everything but the cake.

"No! What happened?" Tee screamed.

"Don't come running now, Big Head," I said. "You are going to have to drive me back home. I am NOT ready to drive. Then, get your car, and go set up for the party. Jo Jo and I will be on later when it cools off. Stay in line and finish checking out."

I shut her down real quick. I could feel her itching to ask me for my truck. And I didn't want her to think she was pushing my fully loaded, blacked-out Range Rover to the hood while I recouped. That was a negative--all in capital letters.

As Tee continued checking out, I centered my attention back on Barry, who was still there, gazing deeply in my direction.

"Well, young lady," he said. "I see you are set to leave. Here is my card. Once you get settled, please call me."

I looked down at the homemade business card that gave his name and title: **Barry Walker, Computer Upgrade Tech.**

"Wow," I said, "I am in need of some computer work. I have some software I'm interested in, but want to clear off some space. I will give you a call."

Barry smiled happily at my interest in the work he did and gently kissed my hand as he said Goodbye.

To make a long story short, Barry and I talked for two weeks on the phone about his past failed relationships and marriage. We shared meaningful conversations until I came clean about being HIV positive.

Then I became the HIV Educator with a million and one answers to Barry's numerous questions, especially as he had kissed me on my hand.

The calls stopped after Barry drained every bit of knowledge I could share on the subject. You would have thought HIV was airborne or contracted through skin-to-skin contact, without an open wound.

I look back at that moment and laugh out loud.

HIV is a disease that not only attacks the body physically but also mentally and emotionally. It tears me to pieces that men think they are doing me a favor. Little do they know being in my company is a blessing.

What smacked me in the face one morning was a statement Joyce Myers made on her TV program. *"When you sin a part of you dies,"* she said. *"Get away from who or what is destroying you."*

I needed to hear that.

Then I had switched to my DVD player and heard Katt Williams saying in his standup, *"I've known me all my life. I can't break up with me."*

Temptations of the flesh...
The real question is:
How do you live without them?

Three

Tiny's salon, where I get my hair done, also has barbers tailored to meet the beauty needs of men. One perfect "Carolina Blue Sky" day, I was utterly astounded.

It was the day I met the love of my life.

I honestly have to say the first time I laid eyes on him I needed to know who he was, what he was about and the big question: Was he single?

A tall medium build man with dark chocolate skin. Just like mine, I thought. Smooth lips and dreamy eyes that carried a smile when he made contact with yours.

He had a bald head with a neatly shaped goatee connecting perfectly to his mustache and sides.

And by the looks of him, he appeared to be clean- cut and all around sexy. Just the way I like them.

"Hey, Tiny," I asked my friend, standing behind me—all five foot and ¾ mocha-skinned inches of her-- with a pair of Marcel curlers in her hand. "Who is that?"

"Who are you talking about, girl?" Tiny said, looking around squinting eyes to get a look at anyone new I was inquiring information about.

"The cutie standing by the soda machine in the blue shirt," I said, kicking my legs.

"Oh, that's ATL," she said, smiling at me as she continued twirling the world out of them Marcel curlers.

"Oh," I said with an interested look on my face.

The name itself let me know two things: one, he was from Atlanta and, second, I had to know more about him.

His "Down South Georgia Twang" tantalized my ears when I heard him speaking and excited my eardrums for more.

I noticed him making eye contact with me as I studied the melody of his eyes. In the beginning, I guess he was feeling everyone out and getting to know personalities.

This was his first time in the shop with my being present and he was making me feel he desired the same thing.

I finally got up the nerve to exchange some social intercourse with him. I was definitely taken by his southern dialect and beautiful smile.

When he stepped outside to take a cigarette break, I followed out of curiosity. I felt an opportunity was presenting itself for me to get to know him better. I'm a forward kind of girl, who doesn't mind going after what I want.

I began by talking about the color of the sky and the wonderful weather being produced in mid-October.

"What a beautiful day," he said.

Indeed, it is, I was thinking to myself.

"So, are you from around here?" I asked--as if I didn't already know.

"No, Shawty," he said, "I'm from the A."

"Hotlanta huh?" I said. "Well, welcome to the Queen City of Charlotte."

I said this with "boast fullness," as if I was the Official Carolina Welcoming Committee.

"This is your born city?" he asked.

"Yes, born and raised." I was nervous about what his next questions might be.

"So, what do you do, Regina?"

I was caught off guard that he knew my name and was interested in what I did for a living.

"I…I'm a motivational speaker and HIV/AIDS Advocate. I just recently published an article in USA Today on HIV/AIDS."

I looked for his reaction, eager to know if he recognized who I was from the numerous commercials I had rotating on TV and sounding out from the hottest FM station on the east coast, My 92.7 FM.

On the other hand, maybe he had been told about my personal context for the cause from some hateful individual. I was unsure about whether he knew my HIV status and leery of what his next question might be.

I leaned against a car that sat directly in front of the shop. I braced myself for the next question I was sure would knock my socks off.

"Why are you so passionate about the cause, HIV?" ATL asked sincerely.

I took a deep breath and remembered what the word says about not being ashamed of God. I knew what He did for me when I was on my deathbed with this disease.

I could not fall into the trap of having ATL or anyone else thinking it was a close friend or family member infected with HIV. Most importantly, denying my Father was not an option. I held my head up high and went into speakers' mode.

"Five years ago I was told I had HIV. I contracted from a man I thought was going to be my husband. My first mistake was having sex with this man and him not my husband. Second, he was not using protection.

"God left me here for a reason," I went on. "I had many complications with the disease in the beginning, but God saw me through. Here I am today in the capacity of serving and helping others with something that was nearly the death of me. Now I educate and motivate others at risk."

I felt as if ATL was not going to be receptive to the overflow of my personal life. Boy, was I surprised.

"Regina," he said, "you are a remarkable woman and your strength is admired for your commitment to serve."

I looked at him with relief and provided an unnoticeable sigh in response.

"Thank you, ATL," I said, "that was sweet of you."

"No problem, Regina. I show love and respect to those deserving it."

My heart melted that moment and slid into my stomach, floating around in the Diet Pepsi I had drunk earlier. I thanked him again.

"ATL," I said, what is your government, if you don't mind answering me?"

He looked at me with that big beautiful smile.

"Shawty, I can't do that."

"Okay," I said simply.

ATL gave me a look that said, 'dang, she is not going to hassle me about it.'

He turned slowly and put a piece of Extra Fruit Sensation gum into his mouth to cover his smokers' breath.

He walked towards me.

"Tommy, Shawty," he whispered.

The sweet smell of his breath melted my lungs, this time from head to toe. I shivered from the bass of his voice, carrying smooth vibrations throughout my body.

I left Tiny's shop that day with nothing on my mind but getting to know ATL better.

His own story hadn't been told nor was I prepared for my ears or heart to handle what was in store.

Temptations of the Flesh…

If you have read thus far, the content has captured your attention. You live in the world of a woman wanting a love for her own. You are wanting more…

*The characters in this book are set in fictional format using real-life issues with the twist I've experienced living with HIV as a label. You will catch on to that later. If you haven't read my first book, **Put it on Paper**, and witnessed what God did for me, please do.*

The storms I've faced are the same anyone else faces without the disease. Some are not the same. However, the bad days are probably better days for me. *Through prayer during the consistent storms, I am still a woman.*

Through my trials and tribulations, I know someday someone will cherish the love I have to give and recognize me--not the label.

Through my triumphant tale of flesh-gripping situations, I have finally come close to finding peace with only my faith to hold onto--and the plush chocolate carpet to cushion my knees as I pray.

I envision, through my petitions, the perfect wedding for myself and whomever God sends my way.

I envision that in time True Love will find me...a True Love chosen for me at the right time, a True Love to share My Last First Kiss in front of a preacher...

kneeling...

together at the altar...

together with the one God has sent.

Four

It never fails. Every time I meet someone and keep it real with them, I get left alone. Oh, well. Life is what you make it--I hear that all the time.

If I were a nasty one I would sex the male population to a severe case of white liver without telling them my status. I may be one of a rare few that do tell others of my HIV status.

Most women I meet believe in "don't ask, don't tell" with regards to being HIV Positive. Not Regina. I give it to the men raw and uncut. I earn a new level of respect for my honesty.

After I tell the men about my HIV status, they each have an incident they want to share, that close encounter with a woman they almost hit, but one of their homeboys let them know by saying, "Don't do it, bro!"

It gets frustrating when you have a disease that man says there is no cure for, and you walk the earth as if you have the letters written all over your forehead!

Women stare at me while complimenting me on how beautiful I am. "Look at you, you are so pretty."

What am I supposed to look like? Pretty people get this, too!

I remember attending a charitable toy drive for my good friend, Cherry. As soon as I walked in the door, I got the stare-down, of course.

Fashionably late, with gifts in hand, I directed my attention to the man insisting on my signing in, including my email address. Thereafter, he instructed me where to put the toys I had picked up from a local Toys 'R Us: a Wii console and three video games.

I placed them in a big bag and laid the heavy package on the huge pile that had accumulated in a mere hour and a half into the event.

"Where would I find Cherry?" I asked.

As he pointed in her direction, more eyes continued to pierce through me as I pranced across the floor in my red and black tight-fitting dress.

Cherry spun around when I tapped her shoulder. We greeted one another with smiles and cool-girl smooches. She swiftly swept me across the tiny space to where her close friends stood.

"This is Regina. My girl." she said. "You know the one I talk about all the time." She blurted this above the jazz band that took up the other half of the winery.

"Oh, yeah," a pecan-brown diva bellowed out from the seat against the wall. It was the very chair I would have chosen to sit in to catch a look at everyone that walked through and stumbled out the door. "Hello. It's nice to finally meet you."

"She is so pretty," I heard another one say.

I kicked up my networking heels, and my Really-Do-Not-Want-To-Fool-With-You face and thanked her for her compliment.

"Nice to meet you all," I said and headed for the bar. I sat down next to a man who looked old enough to be my daddy.

"Well, hello, young lady," he said. "Either red is your color or you make it more beautiful."

"Both," I replied.

I searched the wine menu for my favorite drink, Red Blackberry Zinfandel. A mirror hung over the bar that held its position so all unwanted acts could be captured by those sitting in the area.

I look up, startled to see a woman standing behind me, staring at me in the mirror. I looked to the corner where the women stood.

It was the woman Cherry had introduced me to and the woman who had complimented me on my looks. She was staring so hard she could not turn her head fast enough when I noticed her checking me out.

Now--no gay stuff! I do not get down like that. However, I knew she was just trying to figure out why I was so beautiful and living with HIV.

Men look at me with a lust. To get what they can out of me, they assume I have low self-esteem and think nobody would ever want me because I have messed up my life.

I let them think whatever they want.

At times, I regret becoming an HIV/AIDS Advocate. Being bold and outspoken has it pros and cons. Plenty of people want to spend time with me, but behind closed doors.

I have come to realize that the more open I am, the more people want to know. Of course, I fall into the trap and tell all.

Those who are close to me, and know the full story, are tired of hearing that mess about my being hurt, lonely and heartbroken--especially the ones I feel will pray for my situation.

Instead I am met with comments like "We don't want to hear that today."

I do not know about the rest of the world but I need somebody to hear me. So what do I do about it?

Pray a continuous prayer and have faith that God hears my cry.

Five

"Hey, Tiny," I said, "it's Regina calling to see if you have any openings today. My hair is a hot mess."

"Girl," Tiny said, "you say that every time you call. You know how we do. You know everybody has been asking for you."

"Okay, lady, I will be up in fifteen."

"Cool. I will see you then."

"ATL," I said aloud. ATL, the one I wanted to be the love of my life. "ATL," pounded from my lips without realizing the words had left my mouth.

I was hoping he would be at the shop when I got there.

I honestly have to say the first time I laid eyes on ATL, I needed to know who he was, what he is about, and the big question still lingered: was he single?

I walked into the crowded shop and said my usual loud Hello to everyone.

"ATL," I heard my stylist say, "I need another CD with my favorite song again."

Boy, was that music to my ears. He was in the place.

"Dang, Shawty," ATL said, "I just made you the CD."

"What CD, Tiny?" I asked to get in on the conversation at hand.

"You know the song me and my husband love so much," she answered, "by Tony! Toni!, Tone!"

"The one on the Higher Learning soundtrack," ATL sounded off. "I will burn you another one as soon as I get a break."

"Now that's sweet," I said as he gave me an unforgettable smile.

Tiny called me to the shampoo bowl for my deep conditioner treatment and started asking me about Blue, my crazy want-to-be boyfriend.

"Girl," I said, "he is at my house running up the light bill and flushing the commode just because it has a handle. Tiny, I don't know what I am going to do with this clown."

"Well, Regina," she said, "you know how I feel about you and Blue. He is young, not consistent and, simply put, he is not for you."

"I know, girl," I replied. "Since Blue got out of prison, two days before my birthday, he is killing my pocketbook, eating up everything. He leaves all the lights on in the house as if he is scared of the dark in the daylight."

"Dang, that's terrible right there." Tiny said.

"Yes, girl," I said. "It's sad to be walking dead and not have, at least, a little bit of hope. He got the TV and radio on at the same time, as if he's contributing to paying bills. Girl, I can't get rid of him."

Tiny placed her hand on her hip.

"I know," she said, "he doesn't think somebody owes his butt. This nut blames everyone but himself for shooting that guy."

"Tell me about it," I said. "You know, I had to take him to get his birth certificate, his social security card, identification card. Now he wants me to take his sorry behind to DSS to apply for some food stamps."

"What?" Tiny chuckled.

"Yeah, girl, how in John Brown do I look taking him to DSS for food stamps? That is crazy. I cannot get any. I do not feel right about having a man on stamps."

"I feel you, girl, did you take him?"

"Girl, yeah," I said, bursting out laughing. "I said I did not feel right--not stupid. I have to take his crazy butt back down there Monday to finish the process. Until then, who is the new Master barber on site?"

I wanted to change the subject.

Tiny looked at me and said, "You feel guilty don't you? You know...for all of that happening...and you couldn't control it."

My thoughts went back to the day the worst thing in my life had happened. It was a terrible experience I didn't really want to ever revisit again.

"Girl, he is no barber," T said, bringing me back to reality. "He is hanging out at the shop like you. Ole' local joker, like the rest of them--not working, fresh-mouth bamas with nothing but words. There you go, girl, always looking at the fine one. You better slow your behind down--you know Kool Mo D is home."

An inside joke about Blue...

The girls and I had had a gathering at Tiny's home one day and Blue came in, all out of order, with a pair of black slacks, a white button-down and a pair of wrap-around shades like Kool Mo D wore back in the day.

I say Blue is out of order because he is an official thug, let him tell it straight-street and nothing else.

"Well, if I get my way, here I cum." I said.

"Oooh, you nasty, Regina," Tiny laughed. "Nevertheless, on the real, God is going to bless you with a good man. Be patient."

Sitting quietly under the dryer, I thought about the words Tiny had said: *Be patient.*

I thought about the life I was living and the love that was missing.

After I got my hair curled, I opted not to sit around the shop. Instead, I went home to another dark cloud that covered my life.

Six

I hated to see Blue coming. He did not have a car, lived off and on with his mother. He was always just getting out of prison and a frequent visitor at the 4th Street Mansion--a supped-up name for the Mecklenburg County Jail.

Blue blamed everyone for his felonies, for his not being hired. He felt well-endowed, favored his ways with women--and that he was God's gift to me.

"Regina!" Blue screamed from the porch as I sat in a chair pretending I did not see him walking past my Great Room window.

"You saw me walking up," he said. "Stop acting stupid and open the door."

I got up, opened the door, and rolled my eyes at him. Blue never had too much to say that made sense or was positive. Like his beautiful skin, he had a dark past.

He was called Blue because of his dark complexion. He stood about 6"1, 200 pounds, with a look that's not going to have you calling your girlfriends as soon as you get his number.

His personality was the deal setter. He's an ambitious character in a negative sense. He loved to do the wrong things to make the fast money and that was not what I signed up for.

I wasn't surprised at our age difference. Blue was six years my senior and it is what it is.

"Look, crazy," I said. "I don't like you very much. You need to catch your z's somewhere else tonight. I need some Me Time."

Blue looked at me as if I were speaking Swahili or something.

"What?" he said. "Quit playing and give me a kiss. I love you, girl."

"Nah, Blue, I need this time to reflect on life and put things in perspective."

Blue was not smart enough to ask questions to help the matter, nor was he going to try to figure out what was going on with me. His only concern was he, himself and him--just selfish. This was fine because he was easy to get rid of--at least I thought.

"Okay, baby," he said, "you still going to take me back to Social Service to get my food stamps process complete on Monday, right?"

"Yeah, Blue." I replied, disgusted.

Blue went upstairs to get his toothbrush. That is the only thing he could keep at my house. Take a bath before he comes and wash up before he leaves.

I needed him to think he was not moving in on me. I was so glad he was leaving without putting up a fight.

As he walked out the door, it brought even more joy when he did not ask for a hug or kiss, finally a night--and possibly the weekend--to myself.

I turned on my Bose sound system and enjoyed the new Mint Condition CD. I begin to think about ATL.

Sometimes I would hang out with the folk from the shop and tonight was a good night to see what the business was for a Saturday night.

I picked up my BlackBerry to call Kendall, one of the sharpest barbers in the shop. He was like my li'l big brother, just taller. I am older only by a few days.

Like I said, we connected like brother and sister and I found he was cool to kick it with outside of the shop. The bar and the drink are his favorite past time along with some NFL games.

Kendall is a tall light-skinned brother, with a pea-head. He is a handsome dude with a fetish for Polo, Jordan's, and Asian women.

"What's up, Gina?" he said.

"What's up, Kendall…you still at work?"

"Yeah, I got one in the chair. I will call you in 10 minutes."

"Alright," I said, "hit me back."

While sipping on a glass of Red Rose, I waited patiently until the phone rang.

"What's up Gina?"

"Nothing much, Kendall," I said. "I wanted to see what was going on tonight."

"Oh, we are chopping it up at the Steak House on South B."

"All right," I said. "That's what's up. Your boy going to be there?"

"Who..?" he said, "ATL…?"

I laughed, almost choking on the question that came off his tongue so quickly and with such great surprise.

"How did you know?" I asked.

"Because he asked about you today after you left."

"What did he say?" I said, eagerly awaiting the answer.

"He just asked what was up with you and what kind of person you were."

I did not have to ask what his response was; I knew Kendall had good things to say about me.

"Yeah." he answered. "I told him you were crazy, but you are good folk."

"What's going on at the Steak House tonight?"

"Tonight is my homeboy's birthday."

"Is ATL going to be there?"

"Oh, yes," Kendall assured me. "I'll let him know you asked."

Boy, was I excited. We were in the midst of making history by soon electing the first Black President. I was through with Blue and now had the opportunity to get his sickening, controlling nature out of my system.

I reflected back on what my mom said about my needing a man of substance. I did desire a change in my life that involved me as a man's woman and a potential wife to Mr. Right--and not a Mr.

Right Now.

I jumped in the shower and then took a refreshing, hot, massaging bath for my stressed body.

Listening to Jahiem's song *Masterpiece*, I air-dried, anxiously waiting for at least one of my girls to pick up and agree to ride out with me.

No one answered. Holiday's phone went straight to voicemail and Jade's did the same.

Sky picked up.

"What're you doing?" she asked. "And who are you doing it with?"

I love this girl to death, but she is too inquisitive. She's the nosiest friend I have and we've been friends for over twenty years. I laughed it off.

"Sky," I said, "you don't know me, chile."

"Whatever Diva, I know when you are up to something."

"You right. Come ride out to the Steak House. Kendall and his crew are hanging out tonight. Hold on, girl, my line is beeping... what's up, Kendall?"

"Yo, Gina," Kendall said, "come on out, girl! I will buy drinks tonight."

"Thanks, man, that's what's up. I was on the other line trying to get one of my home girls to ride out with me."

"That's cool," he said, "but if they don't, just come on out anyways."

"Bet I will be out there in a half an hour."

I clicked over to let Sky know I was out, with or without her.

"Be careful," she said simply, "and call me tomorrow."

After I hung up, I put on my earth-tone, multicolored tunic shirt and a pair of dark blue skinny jeans. I spritzed my hair and sprayed a little hair polish before applying my make-up. I accessorized the outfit with gold jewelry and a pair of leopard-print four-inch pumps. I grabbed my keys and headed towards the garage.

On my way towards Brookshire Boulevard I-277 East, I merged onto 77 South and headed towards the south end of Charlotte.

I passed the spectacular view of the well-lit Bank of America Stadium and experienced an "eargasm" listening to one of my favorite artists, Sade, sing "*Sweetest Taboo, In Love With You.*"

I sang aloud as a dual-piped Honda Civic abruptly interrupted the seductive sound of my music player with its excessive race-car sound coming from the pipes.

I pulled up to the Steak House and, to my surprise, I saw Holiday walking across the parking lot with her lover, not her husband.

"What's up Diva?" I said as I pulled up beside the two.

"Hey, girl," Holiday said, "I saw you tried to call me."

Trying to be tolerant, I looked over at Sincere, her lover.

"Hi, Sincere," I said. "How are you?"

Sincere looked at me with uncertainty because he knows I do not approve of their relationship.

"Hello, Gina," he said. "What's good with you?"

"I'm good…thanks for asking."

I know I should say something to Holiday, I thought. *My friend has no business with a man in public—or behind closed doors—being married. I should say something to her, not just let them walk around like its okay…*

But, after I parked the car, I met them at the door and said nothing.

Once I stepped foot into the place, I realized I knew half the capacity occupying the spot. I looked for Kendall, and, of course, he was taking up space at the bar. I walked over to him and tickled him from behind.

"This better be my li'l big sister up under my arms like that," he said without turning around.

"You better know it," I said. "What's up? Nice crowd out here tonight."

I looked around and saw an ex-lover of mine. We used to kick it back in the day in Piedmont Courts. It brought back a quick memory of the great times we used to have. That vision quickly diminished when an old friend tapped me on the shoulder.

"Gina, is that you?" A loud high-pitched voice in a 5'9" long-legged slender body sounded out.

"Trina! Girl," I said, "where have you been? I haven't seen you in ages."

"I have been in Dallas, Texas, with my late husband," Trina said.

"What! Tom Tom is dead?"

"Yes, girl," Trina said, "he died of complications from AIDS last month. It was a hard experience, but he is resting."

Trina pulled me towards a quiet area of the bar so she could fill me in on the details. I was trying to catch my breath as the news had taken me by surprise.

"We found out in '07." she continued. "I had to take him to the emergency room with a fever and flu-like symptoms. They gave him a HIV test because of the symptoms he had. Girl, it was positive."

I looked at Trina in disbelief. I had no words to express the numbness that was taking over my body.

"How are you, Trina?"

She took a deep breath.

"Girl, I am good," she said. "My tests continue to be negative and my two year-old is fine as well."

I could tell she was excited.

"Praise God," I said.

"I am back in Charlotte for now," Trina said. "So, how are you, girl? You look spectacular."

I smiled ear-to-ear and held my hands up, took a step back and spun around like a ballerina in a pink jewelry box.

"God is good, isn't He?" I said.

"Indeed He is." Trina reached out to hug me, but Kendall put a halt to that quickly.

"Gina," he said, "come on over to the bar. Your drinks are coming."

"Wait," I said, "I want to introduce you to Trina. Trina--this is my good friend and li'l big brother, Kendall."

To my surprise, they were gazing into each other's eyes as if they knew one another.

"Hello," I said, interrupting their burning gaze. "Is everything all right?"

"It's cool," Trina said. "Nice to see you Kendall."

"Yeah, same here," Kendall replied, his voice fading.

I was filled with too much news for one night. I could not gather myself together to approach either Kendall or Trina as to what was up with their deep-stare exchange.

I excused myself, left them standing there together, and went to get my whistle wet. The Coronas in the silver pail were awaiting my taste buds.

Big bro knew what his sister loves for alongside the beer was a glass dish filled with freshly cut limes to top it off. Kendall walked in my direction, gloom in his eyes.

"What's up, Kendall?" I said. "What was that all about over there?"

"Nothing, lady," he said. "Let's get drunk. Let's just say old things pass away; new things hide the pain of my past."

"Whatever," I said. "So where is your boy? Did you call him?"

"Yeah," Kendall said, "he said he was coming."

Well, after three hours of drinking and laughing, there was still no ATL. I was cool with it, but my time was clocking down.

My body was ready to relax on my feather-down pillow-top mattress. I said my goodnights and exchanged numbers with Trina.

Since she'll be in Charlotte for while, I thought, *we can catch up on old times—and then I can really find out what that stare down between her and Kendall was all about...*

Seven

I woke up early Sunday morning as if I had not drunk a thing.

"Thank you, Jesus, for blessing me to see another day," I said.

It is a habit for me to thank my Father in Heaven for the blessings He has given me.

But, my mind quickly went to wondering how I had gotten home. I know I drank at least eight Coronas by myself.

I was quickly awakening to the smell of Maxwell House Breakfast Blend brewing in the breakfast area.

Two things I never neglected each day and night were saying "Thank you, Jesus" before my feet hit my chocolate plush carpet in the morning and setting the timer on my coffee pot before going to bed.

I went into the bathroom to wash my face and brush my teeth. I stepped into the shower just as the phone rang. Fortunately, I am able to answer anywhere throughout the house using a specially wired system.

"Hello!" I yelled over the sound of the steamy water pouring from the showerhead.

"Hey, girl," the familiar voice said, "come open the door. It's

Blue!"

"I'm in the shower," I sighed. "Come back in an hour."

"It doesn't take that long, girl. Hurry up!"

I lathered up and disobeyed his commands. At that moment my mind was somewhere else and Blue was not the subject at hand. I got out of the shower.

Looking at the security monitor, I could see li'l crazy sitting in the gazebo, in my self-proclaimed prize-winning rose garden. Such a tranquil site--until I saw Blue fire up a blunt.

I announced my presence through the speaker which connects to the outside sound speaker.

"What are you doing, fool?" I said. "Put that out!"

Blue looked up startled at the sound of my voice penetrating his ears, from my being nowhere in sight. He had been locked up for over four years and was not aware of the high-tech security system I had in my new home. After his Assault with a Deadly Weapon with Attempt to Kill and Cause Bodily Injury in the last house I owned on the east side of Charlotte, I had to move.

At that time, I became caught up in a drama not of my own making and all because of Blue's jealousy.

Temptations of the Flesh...

Eight

On that Sunday, way back in 2006, I had company over.

Jeremy was a guy I had met at a bar uptown. He was a nice dude, coaching for a junior college basketball league.

Once again, I had called it off with Blue because I was tired of his inconsistencies. To my surprise, he was not having it.

But, as I said, I didn't believe him.

Jeremy and I had only exchanged phone numbers and shared brief conversations. We mainly talked about when or if he was coming over and my trying to protect him from the craziest Negro on the east side.

After Jeremy and I saw each other on a Friday night, I ignored Blue all day Saturday. He came over to the house later that evening. We argued and I asked him not to come back anymore.

"Nobody is to come to your house or my 'hood," Blue dictated to me before he left, "It's disrespectful. If that line is crossed, I will handle whoever, whenever."

Next to my diagnosis, that Sunday morning would be the worst day of my life: I made the mistake of letting Jeremy come over with his friend.

Jeremy was sweet and brought us all breakfast from Lola's, a good-eating soul food spot in the uptown area.

As Jeremy and I shared our backgrounds on the patio of my home, I heard a familiar knock at the front door.

"It's Blue!" I said out loud. "Let's go inside."

I could tell his knock from anybody's.

From my Great Room, I could see Blue standing outside my kitchen area window squinting as if the sun was blocking his view.

"I have company right now!" I hollered.

"Quit lying, girl, and open the door. I want you to take a look at something?"

"Naw, Blue, I can't right now. Please, leave."

Jeremy came over to me.

"Is everything all right?" he asked acting like he wanted to protect me.

Jeremy's friend, Juan, was a tad bit timid, but he was trying to get Jeremy to calm down and let me handle the situation which, as it turned out, would have been the best option.

"Yes," I said. "I'll get him to leave."

But Blue ended up shooting Juan.

If I had known gunfire was going to erupt in my home and kill my dog, Sugar, I would have not extended the invitation.

If I had known the situation was going to lead to Juan dying, I would have gladly gone to IHOP for some smiley-faced pancakes.

Blue got a sweet plea and was locked up for four years.

I heard someone say "a drug dealer gets more time than a man that commits murder."

After the shooting, his family looked at me as if it was my fault and disallowed me from future family functions. That bothered me since I am a family person. How does it look for me to not be involved with my people's family?

I got this--all because I said Yes to a quiet Sunday breakfast.

As the years passed, changes came over me and the feelings I once had for Blue were no longer true. But I still don't understand why I kept getting back with Blue and kept in contact with him when he was locked up. I guess it was because he showed me love after my diagnosis.

I always felt no one would love a girl with HIV. No matter how pretty I was--I know it sounds strange--but I felt no one would ever want to be with me.

And Blue, over time, most definitely reminded me of that.

I suppose I did not want any additional drama and during his time away from me, and the maturity he gained locked up, being schooled by the OG's, I felt a little more secure about making our relationship work.

In other words, Blue was a straight thug with a no-nonsense mentality. He made me feel safe. Everyone was afraid of him and he did not think twice about what others thought of him and me kicking it.

After time, for no reason I would pick fights in order for him to leave and, hopefully, stay away. But, it only made him come back stronger with roses, candy and great sex.

Now this was truly not what I wanted and it was tearing my spirit up. I had to break away.

I just did not need a repeat performance of what happened in '06.

But, once again, I went to the door to let Blue in.

Temptations of the Flesh...

Nine

"Girl, you are going to make me slap the taste out of your mouth trying me like that," Blue yelled.

I looked at him with an arched eye and a hand on my hip.

"Do it then," I hollered. "I am not scared of you."

I have to admit I was afraid of Blue at one point. I did everything he requested--from withdrawing money from my money market account for him to buying dope that he messed up.

Three times a day I traveled to the Bank of America taking money out and I saw no return on the investment. He was shopping for shoes, clothes and smoking reefer more than flipping and paying me back.

I thought for a minute he was seriously smoking the product and using the upgrade of his wardrobe as a throw off. It didn't matter anymore; Blue was not getting anything out of me.

I was tired of leaving him in my home, locking up my security system and, then, not able to turn it on for fear of his learning the code.

Here I was now, in the last stage of this so-called relationship, and that was that. I tried to humble myself.

"Blue," I said, "please respect me and my home. Be ready with your paperwork in the morning. I will pick you up a 7:30 A.M. to go to Social Services and get you set for food stamps."

I left off the part that, once done with being

Mother Teresa, I was going to be finished with extending my services to him. I was hanging up being Miss Fix-It-All. I was hanging up caring for those that truly showed no love in return. Everyone is not accepting or appreciates what you do for them. Therefore, I am done, I thought.

"So, are we going to watch the game today Regina?" Blue asked. He knew I am a diehard football fanatic with a Panther Gurl plate on the front of my truck.

"No, not today, Blue," I answered plain and simple. "I am going to the bar with some friends."

I was lying between every tooth in my mouth. I was planning to lounge all day and watch the game alone in my theater room and get rested up to be in his presence on Monday.

"You act real stank now, Regina," he said. What's up with that? I don't like the new you. You've changed a lot since I was locked up."

"Well, you can't expect people to stay the same. People that stagnate do not prosper and I have a wonderful future and my plan does not include doing business as usual. So, please, Blue, I need my space, man, so I can get things in order."

He looked as if he understood, but did not believe, the new me who had once feared him, but no longer did. According to him, I had changed for the worse over the course of his incarceration.

"All right, then, pretty lady," he said, "I will leave you alone. I will see you in the morning."

"Yes," I said, "I will come to you. Have your packet ready with the information filled out and I will get you in the morning around 7:30."

As he walked out the door, with his head down, I felt relieved he had agreed to my request. I thought about the good deed that I was getting ready to do for him, taking him to the Department of Social Services to get food stamps and Medicaid.

What kind of woman are you. Regina? You take a grown man fresh out of prison to the mall and buy him a trunk load of clothes and shoes, get him a haircut, feed him and buy his hygiene necessities. You do not even qualify for food stamps and here you are doing this for a man that once was your peeps. He still wants to be in your company. You cannot get rid of him because he always needs you! That's not a man.

I screamed at the top of my lungs and crawled back into bed determined not to feel the same when I woke up.

I ended up sleeping the remainder of the morning. I woke up just in time for the game: the Carolina Panthers against the Arizona Cardinals. My phone did not ring at all. Not a call from Sky, Holiday, Jade, or even Kendall.

"Speaking of Kendall let me call this man and see what happened to ATL." I said aloud as I went towards the phone.

First, I sent him a text to see if he was up. I did not want to disturb him and his jump-off from the night before. He immediately called back.

"I'm up, Gina," he said. "I don't like that smart text about being face-down, pissy drunk."

I laughed at him and hollered through the phone as loud as I could.

"What happened to ATL?"

"Dang, girl, calm your tone down. I'm hung over. ATL didn't answer the phone last night,"

"I thought you talked to him about coming out to the Steak House?" I said.

"I didn't tell you that!" he hollered.

"Whatever, drunk. You might not remember what you said, but it's all good. Are you watching the game?"

"You know it, big head. Let me get up. I'm going to call ATL and, hopefully, you two can connect."

I was smiling with the assurance that things would fall together for ATL and me to finally meet up.

"Let me go and get my dinner started," I said as a joke because Kendall knew I rarely cooked. However, when I do, it's as if Grandma came over and left before everyone got there.

"What are you cooking, girl?"

"I haven't decided yet. Maybe some fried wings, homemade Mac

& Cheese and some steamed veggies."

"Whoa, girl, I'm bringing some Coronas and chop it up with you. I'll be over in an hour, okay?"

"All right," I said. "Park in the left side garage door and use your wireless remote to come in."

"Is Oh Boy still bothering you, li'l sis?"

"Nope," I said. "I got this with both hands tied behind your back." Kendall laughed hard.

"Okay," he said, "you super, friend."

I chuckled at his response and got off the phone.

Boy, had I stuck my foot in my mouth this time! I did not feel like cooking. But one thing I am is a woman of my word and every word I speak, I mean. Therefore, I headed to the kitchen to get dinner started.

The phone rang as I was on my way. On the line was Sky.

"What's up, girl?" she said. "How was your night?"

"It was nice," I said. "Thanks for asking. What's going on with you?"

"Nothing much just lying back kicking it with T-Bone."

"Tell T-Bone I said 'what it do, boo?'"

"He said 'Hey, Gina,'" Sky said.

"I hear him, girl," I said.

Then Sky shouted so loud my Toy Poodle, Misty, woke up from her nap and jumped clean across the room between my legs.

"What is it, Sky?" I said. "You scared Misty."

She started telling me about the issues her sister and mother were having.

Even though I'm known as the one with the sympathetic ear for listening, best believe when it is my turn I advise with good intentions--even if it means telling the person what they do not want to hear.

So, after the long sad story of "she said, she said," I found myself less attentive to Sky and wondering if Kendall had made contact with ATL.

"Well, lady," I said. "Let me wipe down my cabinets before Kendall gets here. I can't believe I have cooked and cleaned while talking to you."

"I do not see why not," Sky said, "as if you have to hold it in your hands, Miss High Tech."

I was hearing the garage door opening.

"Whatever, girl," I said. "I'll get with you later."

Kendall's baritone voice vibrated through the walls as he approached the kitchen door.

"What up, Gina?" he was shouting. "Where's my plate, woman?"

"What's up, bro?" I said. "You doing all right?"

Kendall reached out to hug me, a case of Corona in one hand and another case in the other.

"Dang," I asked. "Are we having guests?"

I looked beyond Kendall and a petite Asian girl appeared with a smile.

"Well, hello there, pretty lady," she said.

I recognized the voice in an instant. Jessie!

"Where have you been, girl?" I screamed.

She smiled as she came closer to hug me.

"In Las Vegas, girl," she said. "I'm back for good now."

"That's what's up," I said to Kendall. "I see why you got all this beer. Jessie can throw back some alcohol."

"I love the new house, Regina," Jessie said laughing.

"Kendall told me what happened."

"Thanks, girl," I said. "It was for the best. Let me give you a tour."

As I showed Jessie the house, Kendall had already popped the top to his beer and headed towards the entertainment room, my favorite room in the house. I had it wired to perfection: surround sound, 64" flat screen embedded in the wall, Bose speakers, red recliners and miniature round leather tables with smoked glass, cut by hand, placed properly on the top of the table next to each chair.

The closet was equipped with every kind of electronics to give my guests a concert feel. The lounging area gave a stadium-seating atmosphere. Kendall sat down in what he claims is his chair.

"Gina," he said, "I promise to talk to ATL for you. I forgot."

"I know you did."

For the rest of the day, we had a wonderful time tripping off folk that came through the shop, listening to Jessie tell us forbidden Vegas stories-- and the Panthers beat Arizona 27-23.

After cleaning up, I walked them out and said Good Night. I

slept like a baby after a soothing bath and a warm glass of milk.

I knelt to pray for patience, wisdom and understanding. I asked God to bring that special someone in my life and, I prayed, if it's ATL, *"Lord, strengthen my mind and heart for whatever is to come."*

Ten

In the morning birds chirping outside my window woke me instead of the alarm clock. I got dressed in a hurry slipping on a pair of blue denims and a red shirt.

The weather was abnormal for the last week of October, warm and sunny. The leaves had had a hard time turning fall colors and my garden still looked as if spring was still in season.

I grabbed my Gucci bag and my keys while calling Blue from my BlackBerry to let him know I would be there shortly.

"Good morning, Blue. You ready?"

By the cheer in his voice, I knew he was excited.

"Hey, baby," he said. "I am ready. Come on, let's go do this."

"Do you have everything in your folder?"

"Yes, I do waiting on you."

"And Blue--" I said.

"Yeah, baby," he said.

"Please stop calling me baby."

"Ahh, girl," he said. "I love you. Quit playing."

I sighed.

"Whenever I am on your street, come on out," I said.

I hated the cousin he roomed with. Out of all the family members residing in Charlotte, Blue had to stay with the one around the corner from me.

I turned on my HD radio as Blue latched his seatbelt. He wanted to hear what the people were calling in on "Dead Wrong Monday," a ten- minute call-in for the listeners to voice what they thought was dead wrong over the weekend.

I heard a familiar voice telling how a man left his name and phone number and promises to hook up your cable, gas and lights, in a note on a community bulletin board in a restaurant.

I laughed aloud, while looking in my peripheral at Blue, the "dead wrong" in my passenger seat.

We arrived at DSS around 8:15. I walked into the building on Billingsley Road with the ultimate plan: to get Blue some food stamps, so he could be on his merry way.

I was not amazed at the number of people needing assistance but, instead, appalled by the same people still leaching off the system. We sat down at a chair far away from the door and I positioned myself to see all that came through for help.

"Regina, can you double check my paperwork to make sure I got everything filled out correctly?" Blue asked.

I gave him a look and snatched the paper lightly from his hand.

While looking over the paper, my BlackBerry rang and showed an unfamiliar number on the screen.

"Hello," I said, "this is Regina."

"Hello to you, Miss Lady," the anonymous caller said. "You know who this is?"

"No," I said, with no clue to the voice on the other line.

"It's ATL, baby girl," the voice said.

A gigantic smile elaborated my face. I pointed my finger at Blue, and, as if I was in church, I excused myself from the space I occupied across from him.

"I've been awaiting your call," I said. "I am in need of a manager to bring order to my career."

I could sense, even through the phone, that he was confused by the verbiage I was relaying.

"Shawty," he said, "are you alright?"

"Yes," I said as I went out the double doors to freely talk with him. "All is well. I am so glad you called me."

"Shawty," ATL said, "are you with your folk or something? I don't want to come between anything."

"Naw," I said, "you are just fine. You are not going to believe where I am."

I sounded as excited as someone scratching off a lottery ticket and winning the grand cash.

"Where are you?" he asked.

I looked around to make sure Blue was where I left him. I saw him rubbing his hand across his head, smoothing out the waves he accumulated in prison.

"I brought Blue to Social Service," I said, "to apply for some food stamps."

I heard ATL laugh aloud.

"Shawty," he said, "food stamps is what we all need."

I laughed in excitement and explained the awkward situation I was in and what, for this conversation, his position was.

"I need you to pretend to be an interested manager," I continued, "just in case Blue acts a fool. I do not want any trouble. I just feel like my time is up with him after this assignment."

"Assignment..?" ATL asked.

"Yes, assignment," I said, "and once this deed is done, I am also."

He did not hesitate to ask me what my plans were for tonight.

"Nothing much," I said, "just watching the game. What are you up to?"

"Well, I was hoping you and I could get together and watch the game. I bring you a bottle of your favorite drink and we sit, sip and watch the game."

"That sounds nice," I said. "I see Kendall finally gave you my telephone number."

"Yes," ATL said, "he called me 15 minutes ago and told me that you wanted me to give you a call."

I was visibly enjoying the conversation. As people went through the door they all smiled at me as my body language gave off positive vibes while this long-awaited conversation took place.

"ATL, I am so glad you finally called me." I said again. "I can't believe Kendall just now giving you my telephone number. It doesn't matter. I am glad you called."

"I am glad you told him to tell me to call," ATL said. "That made my morning. When he called, Kendall said you wanted me to call you. I was smiling ear to ear: Miss Regina wants me to call her."

I was like a middle-schooler in love and finally getting my way. This time it was the adult edition.

"This is my number," he said, "so lock me in your phone and call me when you get finished with Blue. He isn't going to be there tonight, is he?"

"No!" I said loudly. "You just leave him to me and I will call you later."

"Okay, Miss Gina," ATL said. "I look forward to speaking with you. Can you call me at two?"

"Yes, I can," I said.

I was honoring his request with no hesitation and we concluded the conversation with joy in our voices.

I was so pleased to know that for the first time someone was feeling me as I was feeling him. I headed back into the DSS and sat back down in front of Blue.

I knew I had a fiery look on my face and exhibited a changed attitude. I knew if Blue looked at me wrong, I was going to act ignorant.

"Heifer, you not hitting on anything?" his face asked. I was familiar with that look because when he voiced it, verbally, I could not bring myself to look in his direction.

For the very first time I looked directly in his eyes without fear numbing my body. It was the first time I had control over him. He began to move around in his seat with a look of discomfort.

We sat, in silence, until his name was called.

Later, I dropped Blue off, but, only minutes later, just as I was closing the garage door, I saw him walking up.

"Blue, go ahead now," I said. "I don't want to be bothered."

"Come on, baby," he said in his high-pitched, whining tone. That sound made me sick: it seemed like he was faking and begging at the same time.

"Let me tell you how much I love you," he said. "Let me hold you in my arms today. Let me appreciate you for what you did for me today."

"How much money do you want, Blue?" I said.

"I don't want any money, Gina. I love you."

None of what he spoke flattered me one bit. I was tired of his always being in need, instead of providing.

I was worn out, not having orgasms when I had sex with him, and fed up with myself—especially because I was completely blocking what was in the storehouse for my life.

"Blue, I have a meeting tonight, I said. "I am in talks with a manager who shows interest in taking my career to the next level. Sky and I are meeting with him and one of his staff members and I do not need you around. I didn't tell you, but once I handled all that for you today, I am done. I cannot do it anymore, Blue."

He looked at me in disbelief.

"Come on, baby, I love you. We have almost five years invested."

"Invested?" I screamed. "Negro, please. I invested in your broke-down behind and got nothing in return."

Blue looked at me with violence in his eyes, but for some reason he backed down. I guess he knew I was real about the situation.

'Do me a favor, Gina," he said, "fix me something to eat for the last time? I promise, after I eat, I will leave and not bother you again."

I hoped Blue was keeping it all "way real" with me so I smiled at him.

"Thanks," I said.

After going in the house, I shut off the security alarm and began preparing Blue his last meal. It would be his favorite: Shrimp Scampi with Garlic & Butter-Flavored Seasoning.

I get the shrimp prepackaged at the grocery store, then put the shrimp in plastic bags as if I hooked them up. Everyone knows--but Blue.

I stir-fried the shrimp. For the side dishes we would have rice pilaf, steamed cauliflower, carrots and broccoli topped with a cheesy sauce—an easy meal to prepare to hurry his butt up out of there.

I heard the TV come on in the entertainment room giving me

time to call Sky and let her know what position to play that night when ATL arrived.

Sky loved to take part in my craziness. She knew, once she got with me, laughter would ring from our mouths for hours. The excitement missing in her own life would surely bring her exhilaration.

"Hello, Sky," I said, "you got a minute?"

"What's up?" she yawned.

"I am on a mission," I said.

I reminded her of ATL from the shop and when I had hoped to meet him at the Steak House the Saturday past.

After explaining what went on at DSS, I went on expressing how I needed her assistance in making sure ATL was prime choice in managing my career.

She laughed so loud into the phone I had to look around to see if Blue was near.

"Stop laughing, crazy," I snickered.

"Gina, what about Blue?" she said. "You know that nut is not going to go away without a fight while another man is at your house. You must be smoking."

"I got him under control," I said. "I just finished cooking his favorite meal for the last time. Plus, he agreed to eat and vacate, so I can handle business. Blue is a sure cut-up, but I have to say when it comes to my business he doesn't interfere."

"Okay," Sky said in a slick tone. "What time do you need me to come over?"

"As soon as possible," I said. "You being here is a sure way to him leaving without that extra he comes with. That will give me enough time to shower, change clothes and relax before ATL gets here."

"Cool," Sky said. "I hope you know what you are getting yourself into."

"I don't," I sighed. "However, I do know what I am getting myself out of."

I told Sky to hurry and I would see her soon. I hung up the phone, gathered my thoughts, and reflected on my life.

You are thirty-six years young and you sometimes think you know who you are. You do not know your worth at times and you have semi-respect for yourself. You are repeating cycles when you fall in love with men that have significant others, or worse, are not ready to commit.

I felt different about what was in store for ATL and me.

Determined to make the best of what God had for me, I prepared Blue's plate and continued silently praying for a smooth transition out of this mess.

"Hey, baby, my food ready? It sure smells good up in here," Blue said as he rubbed his stomach.

I turned and noticed Blue in his boxers and shirtless.

"Where are your clothes, Blue?" I said. "Do not start now. You know what I have going on and I need you to keep it moving after you eat."

He looked at me with lust and moved seductively towards me. What a turn off.

"Girl, you know I am not going anywhere. I love you, baby. Why are you tripping?"

"I am serious, man, put on your clothes. Sky will be here shortly."

I knew just mentioning her name would make him run to his clothes, hurry them on and fly out the door.

"Gina, baby," he said, "let's talk about this."

"There is nothing to discuss, Blue. My team will be here and my first impression is important to me," I said.

"Oh, you're ashamed of me?"

"Yes," I said, "and I do not feel for you like I used to."

Blue gave me a look.

"Fake it 'til you make it, baby." he said.

"I have completed my assignment and your time is up," I answered.

"My assignment...? What does that suppose to mean?" Blue yelled.

I grabbed him by his hands and sat him down at the breakfast nook.

"Blue," I said, "it is not the same anymore. I do not feel for you as I used to, and my decision comes from prayer and listening to the amplified voice of God. There is no need to hold onto someone that has freed herself from all emotions towards you."

He looked at me with a blank look.

"Once the deed was complete at DSS," I continued, "I was to

let you go. I disobeyed by cooking for you. I just did not want any problems. I am no longer afraid of you. I must move on, and you are not included in the plans. See God is tearing me away. You are allowing the devil to hold onto you. I can't be a part of that to which you belong."

There was a knock at the door and a massive ring of my doorbell.

"I see your little buddy is here," Blue said.

I opened the door for Sky and kept my eye on Blue as he hurried to the entertainment room.

"What up, gal!" Sky said.

I quickly placed my index finger over my mouth, letting Sky know we were not alone.

"Oh, that joker must still be here?" Sky whispered.

I nodded Yes.

Blue came into the kitchen pulling his shirt over his head.

"What up, Sky. Your girl always trips when a man comes over, huh? Imma leave. What time is your meeting over?"

"I'm not sure, Blue," I said, knowing he would be back if I told him when the meeting was over.

"They want to watch the game also."

He knows I'm up to something, I thought.

"Man," he said to me, "quit tripping. What kind of business meeting are you having that they have to sit and watch the game? Look, I do not feel like hearing the answer. I'm going to the strip club with my folks tonight, anyway."

"Don't ask my friend for any money to give to them nasty tricks!" Sky snuck in.

"Girl, shut up, for I slap the taste out of your mouth," Blue said back.

"Do it then, Billy Bad!" Sky answered,.

"I don't want to hear that mess out of you two," I said. "Blue, please, leave."

"I'm out!" he said, slamming the door behind him.

"I am glad he's gone," Sky said. "That bastard makes me sick!" She laughed out loud. "I do not know how you put up with him for this long."

"Well," I said, "he is gone now, so don't get your pressure up. I am getting ready to take me a shower and get cute before that Down South Georgia Boy gets here."

"I hear you," Sky said. "I am going to rest right here in this seat and eat some of this gourmet meal you slaved over."

I laughed as I exited the kitchen. My mind went to thinking about how I was going to live this day and in the days to come...

You've lived a life in lack of appreciation for yourself, especially after the HIV diagnoses. Would anyone love you with HIV?

I struggled with that question as the hot water rinsed the soap that lathered my body...

I am beautiful, thick skin over healthy bones. I keep the chic hairdos and a good heart. Why can't I have happiness? The virus is undetected. My T-cells are 800. I'm sure to find love, I hope.

Something is truly different about ATL. He knows about the HIV and he still wants to see me. He has a job, a car and he is interested in me.

That spoke volumes to me about what my mother had stressed time after time, "Let a man find you," she'd say, "--one that has some substance."

I got out of the shower with a new mindset:

I am somebody, and I am beautiful. I cannot let my past dictate my future. My thoughts cannot get in the way of my evening with ATL.

"Sky, you alright down there?" I called.

"Yeah, girl, and the shrimp scampi were better."

I heard my BlackBerry ringtone *Who's That Lady* by The Isley Brothers.

I raced to my room to answer, trying to keep my towel from falling.

"Hello," I said as I jumped on the bed.

"Hey, Gina," ATL's baritone voice serenaded me. "Hi, lady, how are you?"

With the biggest smile I hadn't had in a long time, I silently prayed that he wasn't canceling out.

"What's good with you?" I said.

"I am just counting down the minutes to seeing you, Shawty."

"That's so sweet." I kicked my feet up with relief.

"Tell me, Shawty, do you smoke weed?"

"No," I said. "I used to. Do you?"

"Yeah do you mind if I blow one?"

"I have an area for that to take place," I said. "I used to smoke but gave it up."

One thing for sure, it would not be in my rose garden. I had continuous blooms which were still holding on. They can't be disrespected by reefer smoke. I keep that area sacred.

I remembered hearing Steve Harvey say on his morning show, *"Everyone needs a sacred place just for you and God, for prayer and meditation. If anyone steps foot in it you let them know what the deal is."*

My garden area had become just that--sacred. A well-lit pebbled path leads to my gazebo. Hi-Def speakers are built in the lawn surrounded by annuals.

A fountain, in the shape of a large rose, overflows with red-colored water from the man- made stigmas and splashes onto large rocks with built-in halogen fluorescent lights.

In the mini-pool sits a statue of an Angel looking toward the Heavens with a harp in hand. A large gold fish swims peacefully in the water.

I rose up from the bed with the phone close to my ear and gazed out my large window overlooking my manicured yard.

"Hey, lady," I heard ATL saying, "are you okay?"

"I'm sorry," I said, "I must have drifted. I have had so much on my mind lately."

"I hope I didn't offend you when I asked about the weed."

"No…no," I said, "That's okay. I am in no position to judge."

"Well, what kind of wine do you want?"

I smiled again as an uneasy feeling went through my body. I had never had a man ask me what I wanted. I always was the one providing.

"White Zinfandel by Sutter Home, please," I responded.

"Okay, lady," he said, "so I'll see you at 8:00. By the way what side of town do you live on?"

"I'm located on the Northwest side of town. Off of Brookshire Boulevard. Are you familiar with the area?"

"Yeah, Shawty, what street is it?"

I gave him the name of my street and he stated he had done

some installs in my community.

"Exactly what kind of work are you in?" I asked.

"I install satellite TV. I've been doing it for two years now. It's a job, lady, it's a job," he repeated.

"Well, I am going to tell you I got rid of old boy. Therefore, the night is ours. I have my best friend Sky over just in case. But things will be fine."

"Do I need to bring my tool, Shawty?" ATL said.

"No!" I said quickly, my mind flashing back to the incident with Blue. "There is no need for guns."

"Well, I can't wait to see you," he said. "Let me get off this phone so I can get a shower, hit the store for your wine, and head in your direction."

"It sounds good to me," I said.

The hour was drawing close to his arrival. Sky and I sat in the entertainment room waiting for the game to come on and ATL to cross the threshold and embellish my home.

Sky started yawning as the clock drew closer to the eight o'clock hour.

"Hey, Gina," she said, "how well do you know this guy?"

She was smacking her lips as she does after a yawn. I looked at her as I wiggled around in my theater seat.

"I don't know him well at all," I said, "just his vibe when kicking the bobo with customers and messing with folk that step foot into the Lion's Den."

"What in the world is the Lion's Den?"

I had to chuckle at Sky's question.

"Where the ladies dwell in the shop…" I told her. "The men have their area and once the opposite sex steps foot in our territory, they become prey to jokes, and I mean they catch it.

We get 'em hard--from wearing shiny shoes to having buckteeth with gold on them. The whole shop laughs so hard, some of us have tears in our eyes. Until it is someone else's turn. Not ATL."

I looked down at my nails and rubbed them across my raspberry-colored terry cloth boy shorts with the matching tank top.

"ATL is special and always kept his distance," I continued. "He kept a smile all the time and only came in to the danger zone when he wanted a soda. The Lion's Den has the snack and soda machine. He never became the butt of any of our jokes."

I smiled as I rubbed my legs, reaching for the universal remote to turn on the radio.

"Girl," Sky said, "that's my song."

"Who is that singing?"

"Chile, that's Ledisi. I love that song, *In the Morning*. Sky was singing and swaying to the beat.

"I think your 'crack berry' is ringing," she said, interrupting herself.

"Thanks girl," I said, "I must have hit the mute button by mistake. Glad you saw the light flash...its ATL...Hello."

"Hey, Shawty," ATL said, "what's your address? I'm on your street."

"It's 5231."

"I'm out front."

"Okay," I said. "I will let you in."

"I hope so," he said, laughing.

"Be easy on him, Sky," I said on my way to the door. Sky has a way of interrogating my male friends.

After introductions, we all sat in the media room laughing. I was drinking my wine, Sky on the Coronas, while ATL sipped on his Courvoisier.

Sky began to yawn off again so she went to the guest room that she claims as her 'quiet place' away from home.

"Do you want anything before I go to sleep?" she asked.

When she went down to the kitchen to refresh my glass of wine, I decided to take ATL up on his request in an earlier text message when he stated he wanted to taste my lips.

As soon as Sky hit the corner, I tapped him on the shoulder and reversed his come on.

"Can I taste your sexy lips?" I said.

He leaned forward, looked me in my eyes, and slowly pressed his soft lips on mine.

We both closed our eyes and fell deep in a pool of romantic bliss. We held one another and he caressed me gently as he continued to make my body quiver.

Suddenly I snapped back to my initial state, taking back control of my too-soon submissive body.

"Wow!" I said as I rubbed the back of my relaxed hair to make sure it was in place.

I tried to catch my breath, grabbing my shirt near my chest, barely in control of my rapid heartbeat.

ATL looked at me, deeper than anyone had ever before.

"Wow, you are so beautiful," he said.

"Can I ask you something?" I said.

It was the question I dreaded asking.

"Sure," he said.

"Please keep it real," I said. "I do not have time for games."

"Okay, Shawty, what is your question?"

I looked passionately into his dark eyes.

"Do you have any kids?" I asked.

He looked back at me.

"Yes," he said quickly. "Two--a boy and a girl my son is soon to be two and my daughter is six months."

My body language shut down: I had a hunch what the answer to my next question would be.

"Are you still with your kids' mother?" I asked.

"I am going to keep it real, Shawty," he said. "I am not with my son's mom anymore, but my daughter's mom and I live together. We are not getting along very well these days and I dread seeing her. I'm truly sticking around for my daughter."

I looked at him with admiration.

"I admire a man that loves his kids," I said. "It's good you two can live in the same house like that."

I knew it was a stupendous thing to say.

"Shawty," he said, "we are like roommates. All I do is play with my daughter when I am home. I take care of her needs and watch ESPN. I love my baby girl. Her mom shows me no attention and I cannot even remember the last time I kissed her like that."

ATL took out his BlackBerry and showed me pictures of his beautiful kids. He bypassed a picture of a light-skinned woman that looked as if she had three bags of 12" Yaky hair, crinkled with a bang. He flipped it back with no hesitation.

"This is my daughter's mom," he said.

"Oh," I said, "she is cute. Please, then, explain to me why you are here."

He turned and looked at me in a serious, yet charming, way.

"Look, Shawty," he said, "I'm not happy at home. The only reason I am there is because of my daughter."

I looked at him as if he might really think I was some born-in-a-barn-last-night chick. In addition, he hadn't answered the question.

"Negro," I said, "I bet you can guess how many times I have heard that line. I have much experience with another woman's man and all I ask is for you to keep it all the way 100 with me."

"I respect that, Shawty," he said. "That is why I like you. You keep it all the way real and take no junk from these Negroes."

He lifted up his fist as if he was going to give me a pound.

"I'm still a lady," I said. "Don't get the game twisted."

We both shared a laugh and joined lips again.

Not much football was watched. However, we did spend a lot of time talking and, as he kept saying, "tasting my lips."

"I am going to check on Sky," I said, excusing myself.

The TV and the table lamp lit up her room.

She's out like a woman that put in 8 hours building the NASCAR Hall of Fame in uptown Charlotte, I thought.

I did not want to disturb her at first, but I had gotten hot and bothered from the many kisses ATL and I were sharing.

"Yo girl okay?" ATL asked when I got back.

"Yeah," I said. "I am going to wake her and see if she is going home or staying over."

I excused myself again and went back to the guest room.

"Hey girl!" I startled Sky with my loud voice. "Are you staying or going home?"

Yawning and stretching her way out of bed, Sky began to hurry up and sing the old Chante Moore tune, *"Sky's…gotta man at home… and he's waiting there for me."*

We busted out laughing as she put on her shoes and grabbed her jacket.

"Have fun, Gina-girl," she said, "but, please, please, be careful."

"Thank you, lady," I said. "I appreciate that. Let me walk you to the door."

I shut the door adjacent to the garage after seeing Sky leave. I returned to the ET room to find ATL rolling up his blunt. The aroma from the bag of green reminded me of the days I used to smoke.

He looked at me as he twisted a thick bud around between his thumb and index finger. I saw the fine red hairs laced in the greenery as he graded it up fine and placed it in the grape smelling leaf.

"Wow, Gina-girl," he said, "you are so beautiful. I have not felt like this in a long time and I hope we can see more of each other."

I smiled at his choice of words and how he ran that entire sentence together real fast without taking a breath.

However, my mind still lingered on the question:

Why are you here?

He continued filling his blunt with high-priced reefer while sweet-talking me at the same time.

"Where can we go smoke this?" he said.

"Ha," I laughed out loud. "We..? I don't smoke anymore. Come on, let's go to the patio."

I walked him out of the ET room and up some stairs to the second level of my three-story home.

My bedroom has the balcony, I thought.

Quickly changing my mind, I steered ATL towards my room where elegant and lighted red candles scented the room with roses.

As Will Downing play softly through the speakers. At first, the music wasn't noticeable because of the TV sounding out the game through the stadium-adjusted speakers. Our energy overpowered the sweet serenades of good music.

Fresh linen on my California king-sized bed and voluminous sheers created a relaxed mood as an autumn wind seduced the candlelight making the sheers dance.

"Wow, Shawty, your house is beautiful," ATL said. I don't know why I just said that. I should have known your palace was special."

"Thank you very much," I said. "Before my diagnosis I used to enjoy interior design, but gave it up after I got sick. I'd rather keep my home beautiful than fly all over the world. I enjoy the art of living beautiful."

"You are so creative," he said, "mind, body and spirit."

I smiled as I stepped out on the balcony that overlooked the pool. We sat down on two plush chaise lounges. I could tell from the look in his eyes that he felt I had planned the setting and there was more in store.

I took a sip from my glass of wine.

"This is how I live," I said. "I enjoy myself and what God blesses me with. With or without a man present, I am okay."

I felt him looking at me as I was drinking from the glass and admiring the half-moon in the sky.

For the first time I sat in comfort with a man that seemed trustworthy enough to hold my heart. It was a pleasurable feeling to know we had immediately complemented one another.

I can't be wrong, I thought.

ATL pulled on his blunt as I started prying into his life.

"Where are your parents? Do they live here?"

"No," he said. "My dad is in Atlanta and my mom lives in Columbia."

"South Carolina?" I asked.

"Yeah," he said, blowing the thick white smoke into the cool, crisp air. I wrapped my body in the blanket on the back of the chaise to shake the chill.

"I haven't seen my father since I had my stroke and my mom and I--we do not see eye to eye," he said.

"Stroke...?" I said. "When did you have a stroke?"

"A couple years ago," he said, "I was under a lot of stress and my blood pressure was hard to get down. I felt a tightening in my stomach."

A 32 year-old man having a stroke and a not-so-positive relationship with his mom. What good would he be for me? I thought.

"I love my mom," he said. "Let's not talk about this right now."

"All right," I said, "let's go in. It's getting a tad bit chilly for me."

We walked into my bedroom. As I turned after locking the French doors, ATL was standing face to face with me.

"Shawty, I like you a lot," he said, "and want to come back tomorrow, if I can."

"Well, of course you can," I said. "I have truly enjoyed the conversation, the wine, and getting to know you."

ATL wrapped his arms around my waist and drew my body close

to his. He kissed me passionately and I watched as he closed his eyes slowly, his head synchronized with the rhythm we shared.

I felt my body give in to temptation. I began caressing his smooth bald head as he sucked on my bottom lip.

"Ooh," he crooned, "you taste good, Shawty."

I moaned with anticipation.

If this feeling gets any better I don't want it to ever stop, I thought.

I opened my eyes to see him looking dead at me.

"Regina, you are beautiful," he said.

"Okay, already," I said, "you can stop saying that."

I drew away and found his grip was super tight. He had no intentions of letting go.

"I'm serious," he said. "You are a beautiful woman."

"What about your woman? You failed to answer the question earlier. Why are you here and you having an in-house cook, lover, mother of your kid? Why?" I pleaded.

"I want you to understand that it is not like that," ATL said. "She doesn't kiss me like you do, hold me like you hold me. She doesn't make me feel wanted. She shows no affection at all. When we have sex, she doesn't even kiss."

Wow, I thought, *he's laying it on thick.*

I was talking to myself so I wouldn't get caught up in this web of deceptive conversation. The worst way to fall in love is with the tongue. He already had my head spinning off his kisses and the way he held me securely in his arms.

"Okay A," I said, "I hear you talking. I just don't want to get caught up in anybody's mess. I have had my fair share of mishaps with men and all I want is real talk. If you love her and want to be with her--let Gina know. I don't want to waste my time, yours--or worse, end up hurting her. I am a queen and I want more."

"I just need for us to take it slow," he said. "Give me time to put some things in place. One thing for sure, I like being in your company and want to spend more time with you, if you don't object."

"I don't," I said. I hugged him tight and began rocking to a *If You Don't Know Me by Now* remake by Seal.

ATL responded to my hug and we began kissing one another again. We moved slowly towards the bed.

"I can't, Gina," he was saying all the while, "I can't."

"Then leave," I whispered in his ear, "if you don't want to go any further--leave my house now."

What is it that makes me act like this? What deep needs I must have.

He grabbed me tighter and we lay in one another's arms. We continued to kiss and feel each other's bodies.

Temptations of the Flesh...

I unzipped his zipper after unbuckling the belt and taking his button out of the loop of his jeans. He nervously moved my hands away as I continued kissing his neck and running my tongue around the edge of his ears.

"No. Gina, I caaa---"

"Shhhh," I said, "lay back and enjoy. You said yourself you are not pleased at home. Let me take care of your needs."

I handed ATL a condom from my night stand. No matter what I was doing, it was important to protect him as well as myself.

Temptations of the Flesh...

This was the moment I forgot about everything, including my name. I was utterly surprised by the king-size loving he gave from his pint-size manhood. It didn't matter. You know the saying, *"It's not the size of the ship but the motion in the ocean."*

I was drowning in emotions and sweaty from the passion we shared.

When I looked at the clock, it was one o'clock in the morning. ATL was asleep. I woke him up to let him know what time it was. He jumped up and went into the bathroom to wash up.

"Hey, Shawty," he called, "can I come by and have coffee with you in the morning?"

"Sure," I said. "What time?"

"About five."

"Okay," I said, laughing.

I watched him put his shirt on and zip up his jeans.

"You are beautiful, Shawty, and do not let anyone say you are not."

I walked him to the door. He turned and gave me my last kiss of the night and first kiss of the morning.

I watched him get into his car, closing the door slowly as the taillights disappeared.

I leaned up against the door and tried to recapture the evening that had taken my breath away...

Eleven

I woke up early, feeling bright, with the phone ringing. I'm used to the phone ringing at all times of the day and night and am committed to answering crisis calls from women in need.

Whether there are issues with their relationships or they are newly diagnosed, I'm on it. I get out of bed saying *Thank You, Jesus* before my feet touch the carpet.

"Hello," I said.

"Good morning, Gina," the voice said. "It's me. Trina. Did I wake you?"

"No, girl, what's up? I was just getting up for some coffee and a shower before my friend arrives. Is everything okay?"

"Yeah, girl, I just couldn't wait to talk to you," Trina said. "We have a lot to catch up on."

"I know, girl. What are you doing up so early?"

"Gina, I am hurting right now and need someone to talk to." Trina's voice quivered as she tried to fight back tears.

"What's wrong, girl?" I said, sitting back down on the bed.

"I miss him so much, G--my life is not the same since Tom died.

69

We didn't get a chance to get another baby because of the disease being so far gone when he found out."

I listened attentively as releasing the pain made her voice tremble.

"Tom Tom was a good man. Why did this have to happen to him?" Her Southern dialect faded and I could tell heavy tears were forming.

"Trina," I said, "I am not going to sit here and lie. I cannot imagine your pain. I can't identify with how you feel right now."

It was hard to muster up the ability to grieve with her. Tom was the one who had infected me. Yeah, I have to take responsibility, but the truth would have to come out somehow.

"Gina," Trina said, "Tom was gay and I knew it. I loved him so much that I accepted his lifestyle. I have tested negative, but the virus could be lying dormant."

"My God, Trina," I said. "Tom was gay? No, Trina, he couldn't have been. Tom was---"

"Good looking," she interrupted, "...perfect body...swagger like no other. Looks are deceiving, Gina. That was a fine man--tall, athletic and thugged out."

I sat in confusion.

Tom Tom gay? I thought. *No way.*

"Trina," I said, "how long was Tom Tom honest with you?"

"He told me a year after we married," she said. "He told me he knew all his life that he liked men. I felt I could change him."

I was in total shock at this news unfolding before me.

What have my ears heard? I can't deal with this right now.

"Gina," Trina said, "I know about your and Tom's prior relationship."

I was caught off guard by her knowing about Tom Tom and me.

"He told me you two were going to get married," she went on, "but you called it off."

"Yes, it's true," I said.

How am I going to let her know that Tom was the one that I contracted HIV from? But, I didn't know Trina when Tom Tom and I were engaged.

Wasn't it his responsibility to let her know about the disease he had imposed on my life? I didn't ask for this. Should it have been my duty to tell her after they got together? She says she's testing negative...well, that's what she's saying…

"I cannot believe he did not tell you about him being positive," I said.

"You knew, Regina?" she said.

"Yes," I said, "that is why we did not get married, because of his unfaithfulness. But, I never thought it was with men."

"Gina, we are both victims of lies and deceit," Trina said, "and I do not blame you for not telling me that you knew. As his wife, I loved him so much and sacrificed a lot, including my life."

I was relieved to hear her say those words.

"I appreciate it, Trina," I said. "I was afraid you and I were getting ready to fall out over this."

"Of course not," she said. "You are my girl and I love you. I feel sorry for us having to live with this lie."

"One thing, for sure," I said, "I am living and I admit a day doesn't go by without HIV crossing my mind. But, it doesn't control my destiny."

"That's what I admire about you, Gina," she said, "you are so strong and straightforward with it. I keep my head down, wondering if anyone will ever love me again."

"That's true," I said. "I wonder the same thing. But, I figure that if it's meant to be, so be it, and if not, oh well."

"Girl," she said laughing, "I am not going to hold you. I will let you get ready for your morning cup of coffee."

"Okay, girl," I said, "call me if you need to talk. I am here for you."

"I appreciate it, girl. Talk to you later."

I got off the phone, pressure free, but suddenly snapped my fingers knowing I forgot to ask her about Kendall.

Trina is living with HIV! She could have confided more in me, I thought. *I guess when she's ready…*

I knew I had listened closely during our conversation to all the things she was saying.

She admitted it to me in so many words.

I closed my eyes and began to say a special prayer for Trina. *She needs help right now, Lord.*

I looked at the clock and saw I had only a few minutes to get myself together before ATL made his presence known. But, I was still baffled why Trina was keeping her diagnosis a secret.

Did she mean to leak it out? I can't worry about that now. Tender Kisses is about to arrive. I need to be ready before he gets here.

My cell alerted a text coming through. I peered at the phone to see ATL's name shining in the dim light of my screen.

GOOD MORNING. I read the words with a smile on my face.

GOOD MORNING TO YOU. I texted back.

I'M ON MY WAY. OPEN THE DOOR, he hit back.

FOR YOU I WILL, I replied.

I managed to successfully take a quick bath the way, Joanna, a friend from the shop taught me. The thought of ATL's embrace excited me.

The doorbell rang.

"Oh, my," I shouted out, "I forgot to unlock the door."

I pressed the speaker button on the wall panel and told him I was coming down.

I scurried around the room for my red camisole to wear with my chocolate silk boy shorts. I grabbed my favorite Marc Jacobs perfume and sprayed a mist up in the air so it could shower my entire upper body.

The fresh smell of the Columbian Roasted coffee filled the house with its morning brew. I slid across the neatly polished hardwood floor towards the door in my red Isotoner slippers.

Patting the back of my head to make sure no strand was out of place, I adjusted my face for the seductive look I had perfected without looking in a mirror.

With lip gloss shining, eyelashes poppin' and my stomach muscles tensing up at the thought of ATL's almost-touches to my body, I opened the door for the tall dark brother greeting me with a Southern twang.

"Good morning, Shawty," he said, looking satisfied to see what was in front of him. He carefully eyed every inch of my body. "Wow, good morning to you, beautiful."

He stepped back and paraded around me. After locking the door, I turned slowly towards him while he was merry-go-rounding me.

He grabbed me around my waist and drew me closer to himself.

"Good morning, beautiful," he said for the third time, pressing his lips against mine, passionately kissing me and making my knees buckle.

"Good morning to you, Tender Kisses," I said softly as our lips met and lingered.

Magical sensations were stimulated up and down my vertebrae. He looked into my eyes.

"I never would've thought, Regina---"

He paused and started to kiss me again.

I gently pulled back.

"What?" I whispered, aware of my own freshly minted breath.

"You are so special, Regina."

I backed off slowly, cradling his elbows in the creases of my arms. I looked him dead in his eyes.

"I never had anyone to compliment me the way you do, ATL, I said. "It's funny that this is happening right now. You don't know the nights I have come home and prayed for a friend of the opposite sex to appreciate me and say kind words to me."

"Cry no more, Regina," he said, "I am here for you."

He rubbed the tips of his fingers down my face. "Let me get out of here before I am late for work," he said. "I will call you sooner than later."

He kissed me, again, on my lips and winked his right eye as he gently rubbed under my chin.

"Tender Kisses," I sang to him as I shut the door halfway, watching him walk to his company's van. I began to cry.

Father, I do not know the circumstances I am in right now and I need guidance. Please watch over my lonely heart. I know it never mended from the mess I was in with Tom. But, Father, I need You right now. I ask You, Lord, to help me make the right decisions and keep me close. Show me what I need to do. This feels so good, Lord.

I begin to cry even harder.

Let me not be deceived, Lord. Let me not be deceived. Amen.

I got up off the floor and headed to my bathroom to draw a bath in the garden tub.

Sprinkling powdered milk, honey and lavender mix in the water for a relaxing bath and a moment of meditation and peace with God, I lit candles and turned my phones off for complete oneness with Him.

Hello, Lord, it's me again, Father: Regina. I know I just had a conversation with You downstairs but I need to talk to You again.

You know my life better than I. I need You, Lord, to help me understand my position with ATL. Why do I feel this way so soon? Who is this man? I know I need to be easy, Father.

I laughed softly.

You know best, Lord. Allow me peace and understanding. I ask this of You, in Your Son Jesus name. Amen.

After my meditation and conversation with God, I was completely relaxed in the milk bath.

Then it was time to go to work.

Twelve

"Good morning, Regina," my personal assistant said.

"Good morning to you, Ms. Brandee. What's on my agenda today?"

Brandee placed a flyer on the desk.

"*Girls in the Hood,*" I read, "*Presents Real Talk with Regina BoRose.*

"My favorite group of women," I said. "I love meeting with them. What's the topic today?"

"They have some new members and they want you to do *HIV AIN'T ME.*"

"Great," I said, "find out how many new ladies joined the group and T-shirt sizes. I want goodie bags with shirts, pamphlets, key chains, water bottles and the Milk N' Honey bath mix as stuffers. What time is the group meeting Ms. Brandee?"

"At 6 pm, Ms. Regina," Brandee said, pulling already-stuffed duffle bags out of the Education Closet.

"Thanks, mama," I said, "I will meet you at the recreation center with the bags. Call and see if they are serving dinner tonight. If not, call Sky and tell her to whip up spaghetti, garlic bread, tossed salad and banana pudding for my friends in Boulevard Homes. Write her a check and I will sign it when I get to the rec center. Don't forget the tea, Ms. B."

"I promise," she said, smiling.

"Ms. Regina?" Brandee said with an earnest look on her face.

"Yes, Ms. B," I said.

"You are a blessing to many women and you haven't heard this so I am going to tell you," she said. "You are a blessing to me. When I lost faith and did not know where to turn or who to turn to, you were there. Continue to serve, baby girl."

Tears formed in my eyes. The much-needed compliment, designed as a comfort, signaled confirmation that I was doing what God had called me to do. Her words calmed my spirit, even though His answer on my relationship issue was still undelivered.

"Okay, lady," I said, "I will see you later on."

I reached out to hug Brandee tight.

"Now let me go do the twelve o'clock "Lunch and Know" series at Grace Memorial Home Care," I said.

I felt a comforting peace that day. I knew it was because I connected with the Father of all Fathers. I am blessed and there is nothing nobody can do about it.

Not long after I arrived and parked near the door,

I heard a voice calling out my name.

"Good afternoon, Gina-Gina."

I turned from the trunk of my truck to see my girl, Holiday, who is the Founder and Executive Director of Grace Memorial Home Care Agency.

"What's up, stranger?" I said. "I tried to call you after the Steak House last weekend."

I walked towards her for a hug.

"Girl," she said, "I was in jail."

"What?" I snapped. "In jail..?"

"Yes, girl," she said, "that fool smacked me and I hit him upside the head with a hammer."

"Shut up," I said, "and watch yo' mouth. You know better than to call anyone a fool. Why didn't you call me?"

"Okay, sorry, preacher lady," she laughed. "Well, for starters, they kept me the whole weekend. I was the aggressor, so you know how that goes. Nevertheless, I am out and I learned a lesson."

"What lesson?" I said.

"Never trust anyone with your money or your heart," she said.

"Girl, you are too much," I said. "I wanted to warn you at the Steak House. How serious are you about your vows, lady?"

"What do you mean?" Holiday said.

"You know marriage is sacred," I said. "God is holding us accountable for all our actions."

Holiday grabbed one of my bags out of my hand.

"When enough is enough," she said. "You'll stray, too. I guess I wanted so bad to be married that I was okay for a little while. Girl, there is nothing at home, that's why I hardly be there."

"I'm not judging, lady," I said. "Just be careful. You know that Alienation of Affection Law here is going to have old boy taking you and your boy toy down through there. Just be careful."

"Thanks, friend," she said. "But it is what it is."

Who am I if I am doing wrong? I thought. Inwardly I was looking forward to a quiet evening with ATL, but, outwardly, my focus had to be on giving a worthwhile presentation for the women infected with HIV/AIDS at Grace Memorial.

I thought about the new member I had met the last time. The tears in her eyes and the emotions in her voice had overpowered my spirit. I had to reach out and hug Peaches again.

She was only twenty-seven years old and pregnant for the first time. On the same day she learned she was pregnant, Peaches also found out she was HIV positive. She had been married only once---to the love of her life that was now on life support because his kidneys had failed and the valves to his heart were eighty-five percent blocked.

I looked forward to seeing her again.

I would give her a book of inspirational stories written by a group of women I had done a workshop with in Washington, D.C.

At the end of this group's 12-week, hour and a half, once a week session, they completed and published a book of their personal stories.

The book had been uploaded to a printing company in Charlotte and each of them had a copy to keep with access to the site for family and friends to purchase. Proceeds benefited their women's empowerment group.

I was truly hoping my new friend, Peaches, would be at Grace Memorial this day so I could lift her spirits.

I walked in the dimly lit room where the sessions take place and noticed, not only the lights turned down, but candles lit. The heads of all the women from the last session were bowed.

No unfamiliar faces. I knew there were supposed to be new women coming in today--but, now, there were just tears on the familiar faces.

Because of a loss, I thought. *Holiday didn't say anything, but then, someone dies here every day of complications from AIDS.*

"Ms. G," one of the women called, running up to me with open arms. It was Lexy, a thin, dark-skinned woman with big, brown eyes and long, black hair.

"Why did she do it?" she cried. "Why?"

I looked around in confusion.

"Tell me, Lexy," I said. "What's wrong? What's going on?"

Lexy fought back the tears, drawing on all her composure.

"She killed herself," she said. "Peaches killed herself!"

"Oh, my God," I cried. "No! When...?"

"Last night," Lexy said. "She shot herself in the head. She couldn't take it anymore. Dealing with her husband in the hospital, holding onto nothing was more than she could bear. Pregnant and HIV positive! That was too much for her young heart and mind to carry!"

I saw the other women lifting their heads as Lexy spoke.

Calm and a peace came over me.

"Today is the day the Lord has made," I said to them all. "There is nothing too hard for God. Be glad and rejoice in it, ladies. We must embrace one another and not claim that disease."

"Oooh, Ms. G!" Lexy cried.

I grabbed her and held her tight. I motioned for the other women to come up and hold onto one another.

I started to sing.

"They say I wouldn't make it…"

Their eyes got wetter, their sobbing louder and louder. We didn't have a regular session after song and prayer. The women wanted to reflect on Peaches' life.

When it was my turn to speak, I pulled out the book that I wanted to give Peaches.

"Each one of you has a special place in my heart," I said, "but Peaches felt she needed some extra attention. We don't know what was truly going on in Peaches' mind. We are in no position to judge. She was a child of God and couldn't handle the pressure.

"Ladies, the Bible, in Second Corinthians 6:19-20, says *What? Know ye not that your body is the temple of the Holy Ghost which is in you, which ye have of God. And ye are not your own? For ye are bought with a price: therefore, glorify God in your body, and in your spirit, which are God's.*

"I, too, contemplated suicide," I told them.

I could see their eyes get wide.

"Yes," I said, "I had so much pressure like Peaches and had no one to talk to. I went to my Daddy in prayer."

"Yo Daddy!" Lexy called out.

"That's what I call God, too," another one said. "My Daddy." I smiled.

I can count on my hand how many people call God Daddy. Yes, He is my Father, therefore I call Him Daddy. Now, Lord, help me tell them what turned me around, how You kept me from jumping off a cliff in the Blue Ridge Mountains.

As I told my story, I saw the ladies sitting with fists holding up teary faces. They were fixated on my testimony.

"Then, God spoke to me," I told them, "and told me to go to the trunk of my car. I opened the trunk and my Bible was there. I picked it up and opened it directly to First Peter 1:5-7 and began to read these words… *who through God's power are being guarded through faith for a salvation ready to be revealed in the last time. In this you greatly rejoice, though now for a little while you may have had to suffer grief in all kinds of trials.*

These have come so that your faith, of greater worth than gold which perishes, even though refined by fire, may be proved genuine and may result in praise, glory, and honor when Jesus Christ is revealed."

"Hope!" I continued, "I had Hope for the first time. God had a plan for me. After I read that passage I looked up to the Heavens and thanked God like I never thanked Him before."

"Yo, Ms. G," Lexy asked, "do you think Peaches heard God?"

I looked up with tears in my eyes.

"Lexy," I said, "she probably didn't listen."

The room was quiet, but a ray of light was peeking through the blinds. Hope was peering its way into the room and the warmth was felt by every woman.

Each one of us looked at the light shining on us and said, "Thank you."

Because of the suicide, the newly arrived "faces of AIDS" were instructed to go in another room with Holiday so they would not be traumatized by Peaches' death.

I spent the rest of the day with the ladies. This day had been a hard pill to swallow.

Lord, I am so thankful for being equipped to minister to these women. Minister?

Did I just think that?

It was a long day at Grace Memorial and Girls in the Hood ran over by an hour because word had gotten out about Peaches' suicide.

Grief counselors came in and assisted me during the next session. I was amazed at how these tough women broke all the way down over Peaches' death. They allowed themselves to grieve. Now the healing process would begin...

Thirteen

"What a day!" I told my mom on the phone,
Sighing from all I had endured.

"How was it, sweetheart?" my mom said.

"It was a day to remember, Mom," I said. "Enough about me how are you?"

"All is well," she said. "Getting ready for bed, I have an early doctor's appointment."

"Well," I said, "I just wanted to check on you and say I love you. Now I'm going to get a bath and get ready for bed."

"Okay, Gina," she said, "I will talk to you later."

After I got off the phone with my mom, text messages were coming in back-to-back. I looked at the screen and ATL had sent me five messages.

I went into my bathroom to run water for my Milk and Honey bath. As the water slowly rose nearer and nearer to the jets, I began dialing ATL's number.

I sat down on the olive-colored chaise lounge under the bay window overlooking the lake that surrounds the west side of my luxury home.

Tall pillars eloquently surround the corners of the extra large garden tub. Adding beautiful accents is as important to me as the functions in the bathroom. On an open-faced shelf embedded in the wall over the tub sit three large candles. I lit them to calm the day's stress into a tranquil evening of peace.

What makes this room more inviting are the grown-up accents that set this room apart from the others. Don't get it twisted. My house is immaculate, but my bathroom, my throne room, is my secret place.

Just as I began to dial ATL's number, my phone began to ring. It was ATL.

"Hello," I said.

"Hello, beautiful," he said. "What's up with you?"

"I am good," I said, "getting ready to take a bath. What's up with you?"

"Driving back from Virginia," he said. "We had to go up and get five vans to bring down to Charlotte."

"Oh," I said, "That's what's up."

"Is it okay for me to come and see you on my way back through?"

"Sure." I said yawning.

"You sound tired," he said. "Are you sure you want me to come."

"Of course, I want to see you," I said. "I'm getting ready to take a bath and lay down a minute. What time are you getting back?"

"In about an hour, I hope."

"Okay," I said, "I will see you then."

As soon as I disconnected the call, a text was coming through from him.

I CAN'T WAIT TO TASTE YOUR SWEET LIPS AND HOLD YOU IN MY ARMS.

I smiled as I read the text he sent.

I have finally found the man of my dreams. Doesn't your Word say something like, 'a man findeth a good woman?' Am I a good woman? But, how can I be good if I have already had sex with him? Maybe I need to go easy.

The visit from ATL was going to be a brief encounter due to

our tired bodies desiring rest. A long kiss Good Night was sufficient until the morning birds chirped my happy behind out of bed to the smell of freshly brewed coffee.

Five o'clock on-the-dot my BlackBerry alerted me with a text from ATL letting me know to open the door for his morning coffee and my chocolate legs wrapped around his waist.

After talk and breakfast, it was time for him to go to work and me off to the salon.

"What's up everybody?" I announced as I entered the shop.

"What's up with you Gina? You saw my boy this morning?" Kendall said, smiling.

"Yep, every morning," I said. "I am going to get you a fruit basket for hooking us up."

"What it do, Tiny?" I said, walking towards the salon area of the shop.

"Hey, girl," she said, "what's going on with you?"

"Girl, I can't complain," I said with a big smile.

"What's all that?" she said, winding her hand around my face.

"Gurrrrl, I'm just having the best time with that down South Georgia boy."

"What," she said, "let me find out he is tickling your toes with his nose. He already gotcha hair looking like pookie-on-the-porch got in it."

The whole back of the shop exploded in laughter.

"Yep, girl," I said, "slap some Design Essential on my sides and do what you do."

I left the shop late. Tiny was pretty busy so I helped her out. On my way home my phone beeped informing me of a text.

COFFEE AND COOTIE IN DA MORNING?

I smiled at ATL's tactless comments.

YES, I texted back.

But, I thought, *tonight is going to be a night of me, me and me. I have been spending too much time with ATL. I've forgotten half the goals that I set to accomplish before the New Year. It's time for me to regroup and set aside the time and effort to write a novel and join ministries at my church. Oh gosh, Church! When was the last time I went to church and had fellowship with others? Here I am focusing on a man that has a woman and a baby. Should I really invest my time on a pipe dream?*

I talk to myself a lot to try and make sense of things that are going on in my life. It beats telling my business to anyone else.

At least, I thought. *The voice I hear is the voice of reason and not the voices of other people's opinions.*

Temptations of the Flesh...

Fourteen

GOOD MORNING. OPEN THE DOOR.

My phone alerted me with that text at five.

I could smell the coffee brewing, as it normally did, introducing the early morning "coffee and cootie" session we would share.

My vivid imagination wanted to take it a step further today. I wanted to creep into the depth of the situation, tickle his heart and mind a little this morning with my witty way of prying.

I know I should be straightforward and ask what's on his mind.

Here I was talking to myself again.

"Good morning, lover," I said. I was dressed in a red silk nightshirt. I smelled of Victoria Secret's *Dream Angel*.

"Wow." He said, "don't you look---"

He shook his head as if agreeing with the thoughts floating in my head.

"Yeah," I said, "I look good to this Negro?"

"Yes, indeed, you do," he said. "Dang li'l mama, where did you get this piece of lingerie here?"

"You like the way it looks on me," I said, "dark and lovely?"

"Yes," he said, "you look so beautiful."

He embraced me tightly in his arms and kissed me gently.

"Good morning," I said as I stroked his eyebrows with my tongue.

I grabbed his hand and we went into the theater room and turned on some music.

"Wait," he said with urgency, "I have something for you. I made this CD for you. I hope you like it."

"Well, thank you."

I took the CD out the case and looked at the Memorex-labeled CD, wondering what songs he had put on there for me.

Erykah Badu's *Honey* was the number one track,

ATL looked at me with a smile on his face.

"Let me see what else you got," I said.

ATL knew I was a music connoisseur and I was eager to see what songs he had chosen.

"These songs," he bellowed over the sound system, "tell the truth about how I feel for you."

We headed towards the bedroom, the music serenading our steps gliding to the beat of Tamia's *The Way I Love You.*

"Let me find out," I said jokingly.

I sat on the chaise lounge while he went into the walk-in closet to take his uniform off. I lay patiently waiting for the opportune moment to get in his head.

By the time he came out of the closet and went to use the bathroom, I was listening to the words of Jaheim's *Masterpiece.*

"That song describes me to the T, right there, babe," I called.

"All of them do," he said, sticking his head out of the bathroom.

"You must really love Tamia," I said. "Here is another song with her beautiful self. I feel like they slept on her."

Then I started to remember the picture ATL had shown me of his daughter's mom.

She kind of reminds me of Tamia, I thought. *I can't worry about that right now. It's time for me to dig in.*

"ATL---" I started to say, "What---? You put that Jon B—ohhh, my, my, my, my--*Precious Love*!"

He laughed hysterically because we hit *Precious Love* on anything and anybody at the shop.

"Boy," I said, "you got it going on."

"I told you this is my way of expressing how I feel for you through music.

I was intrigued by his playlist and opted to focus on the music; it had my attention more than getting in the depths of his mind. Track 6 came on and a familiar voice rang from the surround sound.

"Is that Tamia again?" I said.

"Yes, it is lady."

I knew I had heard the song before but could not remember when. I got close to the Bose speakers in the corner of my room and adjusted the sound to pleasure my ears with the lyrics.

"I've heard this song before," I said. "Tamia sings this? WOW! What's the name of this song? I have to download this to my IPod?"

"It's a pretty song isn't it," ATL said. "Yes, that's Tamia's *Last First Kiss.*"

I didn't care to hear anything else on the CD. This song had me on lock.

Do these words really express how he feels about me? It would be so wonderful to know that a man wouldn't change anything about me like the lyrics say—even if he could. Maybe he's really fallen in love with me and feeling every minute of being with me in his future...

"Do you truly feel this way about me?" I finally asked.

Here I am, I thought, *getting ready to act a fool and play one of my mind games on him. At the same time I need to be sure he is not playing mind games on me.*

He began kissing me softly rubbing his soft, masculine hands up my spine, my defenseless body soon fully persuaded.

"ATL, we need to talk," I said. "I need to know what the deal is. Call it what you want to."

He continued kissing my neck and my salivary glands went into overdrive.

"Wait a minute," I said, "please, listen to me. We need to talk."

"Okay, Regina, what's wrong? Talk to me I'm all ears." I backed away from him and lay across the bed.

"ATL, we seriously need to talk."

I turned my back to him so he could not see my prying eyes.

I was always told my eyes spoke volumes and were the soul to my thinking.

"I don't think I can see you anymore," I said.

As soon as I said this, the old school song *Put it in your Mouth* started playing.

"What in the world!" I busted out laughing and he apologized for the mix up of the CD's.

"My cousin wanted this same CD with this song on it," he explained.

ATL reached over and grabbed the remote to turn the CD back a few songs to my new favorite song *Last First Kiss*.

"What were you saying, Gina?" ATL said when we were relaxed again. "I mean…we are enjoying one another; at least that's what I thought.

Here I am settling once again, I thought, *listening to the words I don't need to hear. Instead of ATL's words, I should be faithful to the words which are getting ready to come out of my mouth. I am fooling myself…*

"Gina," ATL said, "I am feeling you like crazy. I really enjoy your company. Your smile is beautiful; your words are wise and kind. Please rethink this thing out. What have I done to deserve this?"

I turned to him.

"ATL, you are a wonderful guy," I said, "but I deserve more. You stay with a real, live woman and six month-old baby. What in the world can you do for me? You are not going to leave her. Why should I settle?"

He looked defeated.

I knew my face had a haughty look when I began rehashing the mess I went through in previous relationships. But as my story went on, I started feeling numb all over.

"This is our last time enjoying one another's company, babe," I finally said. "I can't do this any longer."

He turned away from me and let out a long sigh. Gazing toward the ceiling, he placed his right hand on the side of his face. He had a grim look of disappointment.

The song was ending and I rolled over on top of him.

"SIKE!" I screamed. "What the John Brown did I just do?"

I giggled as he tickled me.

"Why you do me like that, Regina?" he said.

"It's my turn now, sweetie," I said. "Enjoy the ride because you know as well as I do, this will not last no longer than it's intended."

"What do you mean by that?" he said.

"You know what I mean…" I said. "Let the music play."

Temptations of the Flesh...

Fifteen

I knew it was time for me to call Trina and see how things were going for her. I was so wrapped up in my stuff I had neglected to call my good friend and check on her.

"Hey, girl," I said, "how are you today?"

"I'm making it, G," she said, "trying to unpack some things and get settled in. How's it going with you?"

"So you are going to stay in Charlotte?" I asked.

"Yeah," she said, "too many memories to go back home. Charlotte is my home now."

"That's great, Trina," I said. "Check this out--you want to meet up and have coffee? Or, better yet, why don't you come over so we can chat, eat brunch and play catch up?"

"Sounds good, lady," she said. "Give me fifteen and I will call you for directions for the GPS."

After hanging up with Trina, I refreshed myself in the stand-alone jetted shower.

Being enclosed in the tinted aqua-blue stall was another serene get-away. I relaxed as the temperature-sensitive LED shower lights glowed red. Water, heated to at least 89 degrees, caused the lights to display red; below 80 degrees, they became blue.

My decision to keep ATL close, I thought, *has resulted in a sudden distance from God who now seems further away. Even though I pray every day, meditate and repent, I know I am not pleasing my Daddy.*

I went to the kitchen to prepare a healthy breakfast for Trina and me and noticed the aroma from my coffee pot was not filling the air as usual.

"Dang," I said out loud, "I need my coffee."

I grabbed my jacket and left for the neighboring Wal-Mart less than five minutes away.

"Jackpot!" I cried inside the store. I found a maker just like the one that died on me and checked out just in time. As soon as I cranked up to head back towards the house, Trina called for directions.

Breakfast would be fresh-mixed fruit, bagels, flavored cream cheese with a dish filled with sweet strawberries and, to top it off-- Granola, Yogurt and a Berry Parfait.

I heard a horn beeping, looked out the window and saw Trina had arrived.

"Come on in, girl," I called from the door.

The weather for the beginning of November was just as unseasonably warm as October.

"What up, girl?" Trina said. "I am so glad you called and rescued me from the unpacking wars at my new place. I was totally not feeling up to it today."

She reached out to hug me.

"Come on in, Trina," I said. "Welcome to my home."

"Shut yo mouth, girl," she said as she looked around, "you selling dope?"

We both laugh uncontrollably.

"Not anymore," I said.

"G," Trina said, "you did the doggone thang decorating."

"Thanks, Trina," I said. "Come on, let me show you around and then we'll eat."

After the guided tour, we sat down on the patio and began to pray over our food.

"Thank you," Trina said as she grabbed my hand intensely. "Thank you for welcoming me into your home. Thank you G, for listening to me the other morning. I needed that. I have something I want to tell you. But, you have to promise me that you won't say a word."

I looked sincerely at Trina and assured her that whatever she confided in me, would stay with me.

"G," Trina said, "I have AIDS. I found out several months ago and I also have lung cancer."

I was stunned by this news. It alarmed my heart like hot grease splashing on an arm. I had known in my heart she had HIV, but not AIDS---and on top of that cancer!

"How do you feel, Trina?" I said.

Trina wiped a hidden tear from her face.

"I'm dying," she said calmly.

"Don't give up, Trina," I said. "God has the last say-so on the finishing of our lives. You have to speak things as if they are. Claim your healing. Speak positive over your situation."

Trina shook her head, her face expressing a reality I didn't understand.

"No, G," she said, "I'm dying. The cancer is eating away my bladder and rectum."

She looked deep into my eyes.

"I'm in stage four," she said. "The cancer has spread to both my lungs and my liver."

A silence surrounded us--even the outdoor sounds of the birds had disappeared. The water from the fountain splashing on the rocks was a distant whisper.

Tears began to form in my eyes.

Lord, I am so thankful, I thought. *This could be me. But, I am so sorry for this to be happening to Trina.*

"What can I do, Trina?" I said. "What about care? Medicines, Chemo?"

"I am by-passing all that," she said. "Mentally and physically I am fine. I came to Charlotte to die in peace, without medicines..."

"And the doctors?" I said. "What do they say?"

"Gina," she said, "they have no idea where I am."

Then she burst out laughing.

Trina had a keen sense of humor, but this was no laughing matter.

"Come on, G," she said. "I'm Gucci."

I cracked a smile, but in disbelief and shock that her humor was just as I remembered and she radiated a glow that said, "This is it. I'm fine with it. I am going to "do me" until. I just want to enjoy life and have fun. Will you help me enjoy the season until the storm passes?"

Temptations of the Flesh…

Sixteen

"Thank you, Father!" I said as I stretched my hands towards the heavens and shouted. "Thank you, Father, for allowing me to see another day."

I feel so out of place right now. Trina just hit me with a double whammy the other day, and here I am worried while she is unpacking her things and decorating her new place and shopping like crazy.

"Enjoying life" is what she calls it and here I am, knowing what I'm doing is wrong, but can't stop because it feels so good.

Temptations of the Flesh...

Another day, another dollar, I thought, *but first things first. It's time for my daily prayer and meditation with God.*

I went to the bathroom and started the water in my garden tub, slowly pouring in the Lavender, Honey 'N Milk mixture. Tears started to stream from my eyes.

I sat down on the edge of the tub as the water filled slowly.

Father, I prayed, *I am in a hole with no exit. Why do I lust the way that I do? Why am I not patient and clear-headed? I need You to help me.*

95

Here I am falling in love with a man who has a woman and, on top of that, a baby, and a six month-old baby.

My turn, Father...when is it my turn to love and be loved? I know I am wrong for fornicating and entertaining this man in my home. I need my focus back, my heart back. I need you, Daddy, I need you now! Please help me.

Lord, guide my sister, Trina. Keep a hedge of protection over and around her as she sorts through her situation. Allow me to be what You need me to be to her during this time. Strengthen me, Father, for the journey has just begun. Heal her like You can. I love You, Daddy. Amen.

My tears seemed to help the filling of the tub.

As I stepped in, I heard His voice say to me, *"Spend time with me and your prayers will be answered."*

I immediately grabbed the phone off the bathroom wall near the tub.

"Good morning, Ms. Brandee," I said, "please forward all my calls to voicemail. I am taking some time off to take care of some things."

"Okay, Ms. Gina," she said, "but, are you okay? You sound upset."

"I'm okay, Brandee," I said. "I will talk to you tomorrow. Call my appointments and let them know I have an emergency and will reschedule the first of next week, please."

"Okay, Ms. Gina," she said, "but two of your appointments cancelled. And your five o'clock is getting the floor waxed at her building, so you are good to handle all that is going to get you to the place you need right now."

Tears came to my eyes again as I tried to figure out how Brandee always knows when there is something wrong with me.

"Pray, Gina," I heard her saying, "God is the answer to all of your issues. Cast your burdens upon Him. It's not meant for you to carry that load alone."

How does she know? Where is this conversation taking me and why am I feeling a sense of relief?

"Okay, Brandee," I said, "thank you so much." I hurried her off the phone. I lie in the tub and hit the remote to listen to Kelly Price's *Healing.*

I need this day, Lord, to evaluate who I am and what I need to do about the spirit of lust I have. I need to listen, to learn what my role is for Trina.

Someone told me a while back to spend some time with myself and have a conversation, to enjoy every inch of my black, sultry womanhood.

I will not stop until there are no more communication barriers between **Me, Myself and I...**

Seventeen

What's up lady? How are you doing?

I was looking deeply at my reflection in the mirror I held in my right hand. I hit the heat button with my left hand to keep the water at a nice temperature.

I am doing well, my dear, and you? I can't complain...

I looked at myself again because I knew I was lying.

If I can't be honest with myself, I thought, gazing with teary eyes into the mirror, who can I be honest with?

You right, sister. Tell me off. Speak your mind. Tell me the truth.

No, I am not going to do that. However, I am going to ask you a couple of questions if you don't mind?

Go ahead.

First, do you love me?

I looked in the mirror and saw a confused look on my face.

What kind of question is that? Of course I love you?

Look deeper into your eyes and tell me what you see. Do not look at the surface or remember what others have told you. Speak honestly about yourself and your thoughts of yourself.

The water continued to rise and bubbles began to creep slowly from the vibration of the jets, surrounding my breasts.

There is a battle going on between me and you. It's a fight Regina vs. Gina. It's about time for you to join your divided heart and mind and become as one. You want everything to come to you when you want it to, instead of waiting to hurry.

I could see myself, Regina, looking quizzically at her dimmed reflection, wondering what the Gina-in-the-mirror meant by 'waiting to hurry.'

Girl, remember when we used to pray before we invited people into our lives? Remember when we used to praise God and attend church regularly? Remember how good it felt to see from "whence we came" and we didn't worry about the idiotic behavior of others?

Grab hold of this mess, girl, and ball it up. Here is an exercise for you. Put on as many clothes as you can. Layer the clothing till it feels like extra burdens on top of your burdens. Now label each one. As you remove the layers, talk to yourself about the importance of that specific layer. How does it fit into the lifestyle you really want to be living?

Put the layers in two piles--one for what are important, activities that include Sundays and Bible Study on Wednesdays; the others go in the trash.

Remember what Mom says to us all the time, 'Pick your battles, Gina, everything isn't worth fighting.'

That's funny, I thought, *Mom never calls me Regina. The battle is not mine anyway-- it's the Lord's.*

Gina, we have been through so much and I know you are not happy right now, but your energy is draining me. I need you to turn to your Bible and read Psalm 23 every day like you used to. I need you to go back to church like you used to. I need you to shout in your living room and have your own praise and worship like you used to. I want you to listen to the Voice that matters and stop asking friends and others the questions for which you already have answers. I need you to want to wait on God for this awesome man of God. There is no need to man-share. Everyone is not where you are mentally or capable of handling your boldness.

You intimidate. Be easy and calm down a little.

Now I'm not saying you should change who you are, but be the best at what you do and allow no one to distract you from your purpose. Now, here is my battle with you…

I sat up straight in the tub.

I don't want you to be off course. You are rushing what you have no control over. God's timing is not at your beck and call. It's when He is ready, when you are ready to receive it. Now, you let that marinate.

I know you love serving the community, but you are so caught up in what you want now. Instead, you need to wait—to wait for what's good for you later.

Continue the fight for others like you say you want to. Start a new chapter in your life.

I could see a big smile breaking out on my reflection in the mirror.

Own your positive power and don't misuse it. Those that know you know the truth. Those that don't don't need to see that side of you.

I know who God is, and you most definitely know, so act accordingly. He will deliver the peace you desire, as well as the perfect man when you are equipped to receive him. Remember, God may be waiting on you to get right.

You know I don't need a lot of words to make a statement, but I want you to know I love you and we will get through this tough place. Let's go to God in prayer.

I could see Regina's hand reach out to join Gina's in the mirror.

Then, I put the mirror down and placed my hands gently together. Heart and tears began to release the enemy within me, the part of myself I now knew I could only overcome by being honest with me, myself, and I.

Lord, I now prayed as a whole person, *this battle is what many face everyday but neglect to search for within. Today is a beginning to ending the confusion I face. I keep slipping back into a state of old, familiar territory and do not like it there. As a woman searching for so much, I need to step back and let what I am looking for come to me from You.*

Waiting patiently is hard for many and easy for most--or so they say.

I knew this conversation with my inner self would become the first step to my healing.

This therapeutic process--admitting my faults and deciding to work on the things that cause me to forsake my Lord--was a start to my new beginning.

I am a work in progress.

A valley is what you make it. But, while in that valley state, I will make the best of it until the better comes.

Eighteen

"Hey, Gina, where you been?" Tiny said as I walked into the shop.

Even though my hair had suffered during my rededication, I needed the time off from everyone.

"Girl, I have been trying to get myself together," I said.

Tiny stopped polishing the shampoo bowl to perfection and slowly walked over to me, placing her hand on my shoulder.

"Girl," she said, "what's going on?"

Tears began to stream down my face.

"I'm at my wits' end, girl," I said. "I am frustrated, hurt, and lonely—and, girl, I am mad as hell!"

Tiny's eyes widened at my never-seen emotions displayed before her.

"Come on, sweetie," she said, "In my office."

She took me by the arm and sat me down.

"Regina, I need you to get hold of yourself. What is wrong? Talk to me, friend, I can't help you like this."

I continued crying out of control as Tiny rubbed my perfectly shaven hair.

"Do what you have to do, girl," Tiny said. "Get it out. Cleanse the mess that's polluting your mind, body and soul."

"I'm tired, Tiny," I said. "I can't go on like this."

She looked confused.

"Sweetie," she said, "is you in a financial situation?"

"No," I said, shaking my head. "Tiny, my life... Tiny, it's my life. I am not at all happy right now."

"Wait a minute," Tiny said, turning and shaking her head, her right index finger up in the air. "You are not happy with your life? Gina, you have a lovely home with every amenity unknown to man. You drive the finest cars; have the perfect career--which you love. What is it, sweetie? Are you discouraged about having kids again?"

"No," I said, "I'm not talking about kids or the material things. Those things do not make me happy; they keep my mind off things that really matter. I'm not really sure if I want kids or not."

Tiny looked even more confused.

"Well, sweetheart," she said, "What is it that's bothering you? Has ATL disrespected you?"

I knew just the thought of me being hurt by any man made Tiny's skin cringe.

"No," I said, "ATL has not done anything to hurt me. It's me who is hurting me. He has a woman and a six month-old baby girl."

"WHAT?" Tiny yelled. "Dang girl you---what in the world, you...? Never mind. Go ahead. I am here to listen to you."

I knew a lot of my erratic disposition had to do with Trina's situation: I had not yet heard the answer from my Daddy on how to handle it. I had sworn myself to secrecy and I dared not betray her trust.

But, I also didn't want to talk too much about ATL without looking foolish.

"Tiny," I said, "ATL has a girlfriend and she is the mother of his daughter. I'm handling the situation. I am thinking like a big girl, but I have fallen in love."

Tiny looked at me in disbelief as I told her about the choices I had been making and had just bluntly confessed. I could tell she was absorbing me, a woman she thought was put together well, a woman who taught, led by example and had many wanting to be like her.

This woman before her was not the Regina she knew. I was acting like a woman who couldn't get a man, so I was settling for someone else's.

"I know what you are thinking," I said, picking up my things, getting ready to storm out the door, "and I'm sorry, but it is what it is."

Tiny stood in front of me, struck dumb by what she had just heard.

As I left the shop, I caught a glimpse of her in the mirrors lining the walls. She had thrown her hands up as tears streamed down her face.

She was looking towards the heavens and praying--for me.

Temptations of the Flesh...

Nineteen

Thanksgiving was right around the corner, and preparing the menu was like making a cake. Spending time with family and then with close friends visiting from many parts of the South was a holiday complete.

ATL had already invited himself to dinner. That just added a scoop of ice cream to the already delectable occasion. He was excited about going in to work after telling his woman that he had to work extra late.

"She can't cook," he said, 'and she doesn't keep house well, plus we get a lot of service calls during the holidays. No one wants their service interrupted during NFL football on Thanksgiving Day."

"Keep whatever goes on between you two between yourselves and your house," I said. I had started being adamant about less conversation on his home life until he bought up marriage.

Spending the holidays with someone special was a first. I never had that opportunity and was sure this would be the year. For the first time in the history of dating I was having a man over for the holidays and it showed.

I felt a vibration from my purse.

"Hello," I said, "this is Regina."

"Hey, lady," I heard Tiny say, "what's going on with you? I was calling to make sure you were okay. You stormed out mighty fast on me the other day."

"I'm good, Tiny," I said. "Please don't judge me, friend. I just got caught up. He promised me that after Christmas he was leaving her. He wants to be there for the baby's first Christmas. You can understand that, can't you?"

"Regina," she said, "get you together, lady. You know we are friends and I love you dearly, like a sister. But don't count on him doing that."

"I am not as stupid as I sound Tiny," I said, "but it feels so good. Let me enjoy this moment."

"All right," she said, "I hope you know what you are getting yourself into, because you know how you get when things don't go your way."

"I will be just fine," I said. "Watch and see."

UGGGGHHH! Lord, help me, why do I continue to fall for the least of the best? The very few that are worth having are already in the hearts of others. Who am I fooling? I can't ponder on that right now, I have a big meal to prepare in a couple of days and I don't want the interruption of anything or anyone to have me in a funk. Let me call my girl, Trina, and see what is up with her.

I was shaking my head as I dialed Trina's number.

"Hi, Trina," I said. "What's good with you, mama?"

"Hey lady," she said, "I am in Dallas putting some loose ends together."

"Wow, I didn't know you were going to Dallas. When did you leave?"

"I left late yesterday evening. All is good. I had to get the house cleaned up and get Tom Tom's stuff to his family and things he wanted donated to the organization where he was a client."

"Okay" I said. "Well, what are you doing for Thanksgiving? I want to put you on the evening guest list."

"Go ahead and pencil me in, girl," Trina said, "I need a laugh and some cocktails in me right about now. This is harder than putting him in the ground."

"I'm so sorry you are feeling down right now, lady," I said. "You know who our God is and He is not going to allow nothing to happen that isn't supposed to."

I took the phone from my ear and looked at my BlackBerry.

"Take your own advice," I whispered.

After calling all the best girls in the world I had my menu in order and decided to turn on some sweet sounds of Mary J. Then, I typed something sweet on each of their place cards:

Placing my order at The House of Prayer, my Secret Closet: May I have an order of patience? *No charge.* May I have a side of wisdom? *No charge.* Please give me a scoop of understanding? *No charge.* Oh, that fresh pan of trust please? *No charge.* One more thing and I will get out your way; may I please have another order of everything for my friends with an extra large of that red stuff? *That's love...No charge.*

It's in my nature to go the extra mile for my friends. I love letting them know they are loved and appreciated, not only by me, but, most of all, by God...

Twenty

"Hey, Sweetheart, how are you today?"

It was ATL.

"I'm at my best," I said. "No complaints so far. How are you today, dark and lovely?"

"I would be doing a lot better if you say it's okay to come over for a minute." He sounded reluctant.

"For a minute..?" I frowned.

"Yeah," he said, "I'm supposed to be going to the Walgreen's to get some Pedialyte for the baby. She isn't feeling well. I think it's her teeth. She is going through Pampers like crazy. Cranky as ever and won't eat anything."

"Yeah, probably are her teeth" I said.

As long as it's the baby, I can cope, I thought. *I hate being away from ATL and he knows it. He's made it his business to keep me pleased.*

"Okay," I said, "come on through so you can get back and tend to the little one."

The bell rung shortly after the call was disconnected.

I was lounging in a red silk nightshirt that had slits on the sides showing off my thighs.

This nighty will tempt his tummy.

I remembered the old man at the bar who said, "Either red is your color or you make it look beautiful..."

I knew my body language spelled out both. I smiled at myself in the mirror on my way to the door.

Temptations of the Flesh...

"Dang, girl," ATL said as I opened the door.

The candles were burning, reflecting light off the silk nighty--like fire.

"Wow," ATL said again, "you look amazing." He rubbed the material as it slid softly through his fingers.

"Thank you very much, sweetie," I said.

I wrapped my arms around his neck and commenced to kiss him slowly. I felt a bulge in his pants and, even in the midst of the kiss; I felt my mouth tighten in a knowing smile.

Then I felt another vibration against my side and ATL immediately paused to look at his BlackBerry.

"Shawty" he said, "this is my daughter's mom. Let me take this call."

He quickly went back out the door to speak to her in private.

I'm losing the mood of this moment of seduction, I thought. As ugly as it was, I knew I had been fixated on making the business complete.

Soon ATL slid back through the door beginning to kiss me, expecting to take up where we left off.

"Baby," he crooned, "don't be mad, but she is tripping and she has every right. I should have been back by now."

"It's cool," I said.

I stepped back and rubbed my side, sliding the red tantalizer which ran down my thighs a little higher.

"Go home," I said, "take care of the baby. I will holler at you tomorrow morning."

ATL kissed me and walked out the door. Quickly, he turned around and kissed me again, passionately.

Surely he's letting me know he appreciates my understanding, I thought.

I peeked out the window, watching him drive off in a hurry.
I shook my head.

Hitting the remote to listen to the CD ATL had made for me;
I searched for Track 6, Tamia's *Last First Kiss* to serenade me, alone,
for the rest of the night...

Twenty-one

"Girl, you did that!" Jade said as she finished off the collard greens and dressing from her plate.

"Yes, Regina, you put your foot in that meal and the house decorated so beautiful," Holiday sighed.

I knew it was.

Lights, from two gold pots of red poinsettias, twinkled and greeted my guests. Garlands, with lights intertwined, trimmed all the doorways, inside and out.

Inside, red candles flickered and mixed with the scent of cinnamon. The smooth sounds of jazz relaxed the atmosphere.

Collard greens, cabbage mixed with okra, corn bread, dressings, turkey, rice, Mac and Cheese, potato salad, cakes, pies, tea and wine were among the abundance served.

"Thanks, ladies," I said, "glad you enjoyed it."

But I was plenty upset because of ATL's no show.

"Let us retire to the Entertainment Room and look at some old pictures," I said.

"Retire?" Sky said. "Y'all get ya asses up and let's go look at these photos from back in the day!"

"Dang, Sky, you have a potty mouth, girl," Holiday said.

"Ain't nothing changed," Sky said. "I'm still rough around the edges. I'm y'all back up if anyone acts a donkey on you females. We all can't be booshie."

My ladies burst out laughing at Sky and her crazy remarks, while thanking me for a well put together Thanksgiving dinner and the special gifts. Each one of them had received a present with a card attached telling why I was so thankful for their presence in my life...

"What's the deal between you and ATL?" Sky asked later, a glass of Sangria in her hand.

All of us were seated comfortably in the stadium seats. We had been looking at pictures from our days at Garinger High School.

The ladies looked to me--beamed in "on pause" from our shared memories. I knew they were waiting for my response—a response to everyone else's unasked question: *What's the deal between you and ATL?*

"We are...I don't know..." I said. "He was supposed to come today and didn't show up."

I know the expression on my face looked dismal.

"ATL has a woman and six month-old baby girl, ladies," I said. "He is a pure romantic and he touches every nerve in my body and relaxes me to a comfort zone I truly don't want to give up."

Holiday looked angry.

"Girl," she said, hastily, "what the hell are you talking about?"

"I know, Holiday." I said.

"No, you don't know." she said. "You know you deserve better, but you messing with a man with a family? Is he married?"

"No," I said, "he is not married. But, girl, I am totally pissed he didn't show up today. And how in the world can you talk?"

"What the hell did you expect?" Jade said. "This man has a family and you are a home wrecker."

Everyone started laughing in agreement that I was out of order messing with a man that was living with a woman and had a baby involved.

"I know, friends," I said. "I respect your honesty and quick chastisement right now, but I don't need to hear it right now."

"Yes, the hell you do!" Sky said. "This is some wacka-flocka-flame."

"WHAT!" Everyone screamed out in laughter.

"Okay, okay," Sky said. "Didn't you all just say I curse too much?"

"You right," Holiday said, taking a sip on her wine.

"Look friend," she said, moving over towards me, rubbing my shoulder. "You get what you give. You expect for this brother to leave this woman and they have a new baby? You are mistaken. Fall back and let him make the necessary decision on what he wants because I have a funny feeling this is going to end and it's not going to end well. So don't fall for the Okie- Doke and get your heart twisted and set back in a depressed state over love that wasn't meant for you in the first place."

By then, I had tears in my eyes.

I thanked my friends, my true friends, for not judging. At the same time, I knew they were keeping it 100 with the right thing to do...even though it felt good.

Temptations of the Flesh...

Twenty-two

I woke early to master the art of Black Friday shopping, the day after Thanksgiving sales.

But ATL put a halt to that with his phone call.

"Good morning, Shawty," I heard him say. "I hope you aren't mad at me for not showing up. I ended up working late and when I got off it was hard to get away."

The chocolate skin on my face went into a funky scrunch, but I faked the funk.

"It's cool," I said. "I understand."

"Would you like to go out for lunch today?" he asked.

"Yes," I said, "I would love to. Let me go to the mall and catch some of the sales and meet you at the house around eleven."

"Okay, Lady in Red," he said. "I will see you later."

ATL made a kissing sound and I caught it through the phone, feeling a tingle inside.

I took care of my shopping and came home to personally wrap the gifts for my family and friends.

I was tying the perfect bow when I was startled by the doorbell.

There was ATL. He was standing with a bouquet of red roses. My face lit up with a smile and I reached out to hug him.

"Thank you," I said, "these are beautiful." I breathed in the fragrance from the petals.

"Just like you, Woman in Red," ATL said. "You ready to go?"

"Yep," I said, "let me grab my purse and phone."

We headed out with no clue to what would be on our lunch menu. Once in the car, I suggested Portofino's, an Italian restaurant with garlic knots to die for. We decided to order out.

We walked into the restaurant, holding hands, and sat hungry and trying to wait patiently for our order.

"I'm going back to the car," I said to ATL. "I'm tired from the early morning shopping."

Earlier that morning ATL's parked car was hit by a reckless driver on his job and he was using a rental, a tiny compact car.

Sneak a peek in the glove compartment, my woman's intuition told me.

I opened the glove drawer and saw only a piece of paper and a car manual.

Grabbing the piece of paper, I saw the official name of "her," the other woman, the one known as the main squeeze.

"Imani Raye," I said aloud, looking towards the door of the restaurant to see where ATL was.

Still waiting inside, I thought.

I pulled out my BlackBerry and began typing in the address and telephone number for Imani Raye. The insurance and car were in her name.

Light bulbs were ringing left and right. I had no idea what was coming over me. I felt the need to have this information: for security, for bribe, for any means necessary for the comfort of my heart.

Smoothly, I put the paper work back in the glove compartment and lay back in the seat as if I were resting.

Soon, out of my peripheral, I saw ATL coming and, lifting my head, I made sure nothing looked suspicious.

ATL sat the pizza in the back seat.

"Are you okay?" he asked me.

"Everything is fine, babe," I said. I rubbed the back of his neck. "Never be dumber than the situation at hand."

He looked confused.

I know he thinks about my little quotes when he's alone, I thought.

On the ride back, I used MapQuest to find the distance from "her" house to mine. And was surprised how close we lived to one another--four minutes and seven seconds away.

"Wow!" I whispered.

"You say something, Regina?" ATL said.

"No," I lied, "just checking my text messages from my girl Sky. That girl is crazy."

Laughing at my lies, I felt myself slowly slipping into a mode that I felt I had buried a long time ago.

Either he is going to love me...or somebody is not going to get their way, I thought.

Temptations of the Flesh...

Twenty-three

"Hey, Regina, what's going on, girl?"

I knew Kendall was eager to talk to me. I knew he wanted to find out how things were working out between me and ATL.

"Nothing much," I said. "Kendall, I am so glad you called. I have been meaning to ask you a question for the longest and every time I see you it slips my mind."

"What's good?" he said. "Tell me what is on your mind."

"Trina is on my mind," I said. "How well do you know her? What is going on with you and her or what has already happened?"

"Man, Gina," he said, "that's a throwback, girl. I will tell you, but not over the phone. I'm not too far from your house, so I will use my key."

"Okay, man," I said, "come on, I'm waiting."

Soon I heard the jingle of the keys: Kendall was in the foyer.

"Big head," he called, "where are you?"

"Here I am," I called from a chair in the living room. "Now let's talk about Trina."

"Gina," he said, standing in the entry, "I trust you, girl, but don't you let this go any further than this room right here."

"Well," I said, "let's take it to the kitchen and sit down over something to snack on."

I led the way into the kitchen and pulled out a meat tray, spread, and bread for the two of us.

"Talk to me, Kendall," I said.

"I know you wanted to know what the deal was with Trina," he said, "and I made it my business to not say nothing until the time was right. I hoped and prayed you didn't ask me any questions about that mess."

I was confused but patiently waited for the answer to my question.

"Tom used to be one of my workers back in the day," Kendall continued. "We pushed big-time dope. He was my favorite trafficker. He made every shipment on time and without any problems, except…"

Kendall paused to keep his composure.

"I was notified Tom was in medical care at the airport on the way back from a drop," he continued. "He always drove to the destinations and made the drop and flew back First Class. I was the last number he had dialed out in his phone and they contacted me. I drove to the airport with no problem and no second thought this might be a set up. I trusted Tom and he trusted me. When I got there I noticed Tom was smaller than usual. It looked as if he wasn't eating well and neglecting himself, being on the go all the time. Boy was I surprised."

I slid a plate to Kendall with a sandwich and pickle slices. Then I hunched over the island and rested my head on my fist.

"Tom looked at me," Kendall continued, "and told me he was dying, that he had AIDS. I couldn't do anything but stand there with cement feet. He told me how he got it and how long he had it, Gina."

I looked up.

"Tell me something I don't know, Kendall."

"Gina, baby," he said, "you wanna sit down for this one."

My confusion changed to frustration.

"Damn you, Kendall!" I screamed, beating my fist on the counter top. "What in the hell is going on? Why are you acting so strange?"

Something isn't right, I thought, anticipating the truth. *Ever since the encounter at the Steak House, I've known...I have to know--no matter what.*

Kendall took a deep breath, and then bluntly exhaled.

"Trina is transgender," he said.

Silence smothered the kitchen. I looked at Kendall, waiting on the punch line to the sick joke he just told.

"What?!" I said. I shook my head as if fire was exploding from my ears.

"The year before you met Trina officially," Kendall said, "she... he, whatever it is, had a lot of work done to make the transition into womanhood. Man, I don't want to talk about this mess!"

"You better tell me why the hell I got this shit, Kendall. And NOW!" I screamed.

"Well," he said, "Tom Tom was gay, man, and he loved Trina. I wasn't down with that gay stuff! I just loved the fact that Tom loved making money. What he did with it was his business."

I listened with tears in my eyes about Trina, my friend, once named Terrance Michaels.

"How did I not know?" I asked.

"Hell, baby girl," Kendall said, "don't feel bad. I almost talked to her until Tom started laughing and told me the truth. He confided in me a long time ago, G baby."

He paused for a minute.

"That's how he contracted the disease," he said. "I never forgave Trina for that and I hope you are not mad at me for not telling."

"But how..?" I said. "Why..? I need a drink."

I pulled a bottle of Moscato out the fridge and popped the screw for the very first time ever.

How did I miss the signs? Trina is a man? Is a man now a woman? That explains a lot of the excessive plane rides out of the country Tom Tom made during our last year together. I need to talk to Trina.

"I am so pissed at you," I said to Kendall as I walked him to the door, "for not letting me know about this early on. You have failed to be a true friend. My life was in your hands, Kendall. All you had to do was say something. But all you cared about was your dope money and your precious white girl."

My eyes were full of tears and I looked Kendall dead in his eyes.

"I love you, man," I said with a quiver in my voice, "but how dare you tell me not to be mad you almost messed with her?"

I looked at him with disgust, wondering who was standing before me.

"I don't want to see you for a while, man," I said. "Stay away from me. I cannot believe you have hurt me to this level. You kept this away from me all these years and didn't say a mumbling word."

Kendall's eyes began to water.

He knew this day would come, sooner rather than later, I thought, *and now was the time he wished yesterday was already here.*

He leaned over and grabbed me, kissing me on the forehead.

"I love you," he said. "I understand."

And then he walked out of the house.

Twenty-four

I stayed secluded from my family and friends for a minute. I didn't answer any phone calls and hadn't been to the salon for my weekly hair-do.

Finally, I allowed Sky in for a brief conversation.

"Heifer," she said, "what is going on with you? Everyone is calling me about where you are and what's going on and you aren't answering calls. I was about to kick this damn door in if you wouldn't answer this time. I've been here over a hundred times, chick. What's the deal?"

"What am I to say, Sky?"

"I don't know," she said, "but you need to say something--with your hair all over your head and looking like you haven't showered in days. Has ATL done something to you? Gina, you have sunk into a state of depression again. Girl, this isn't good. What is going on? You are scaring me."

I knew I looked crazed with my hair announcing WASH ME. My eyes were swollen and red from crying.

As we sat and talked, I rocked back and forth

"How did I miss the signs?" I kept saying over and over again.

Sky was getting frightened now and grabbed me.

"What is going on?" she said.

"Sky," I finally said, from the overflow of my emotions. "Tom was gay, girl."

"Hell, tell me something I don't know," she said.

I sucked up my tears and looked at Sky.

"You knew, too?" I said.

"I don't know anything," she said. "You just confirmed it, though. I always felt Tom had a little sugar in his tank girl. It is what it is."

This was all too much for me. Now another friend was confirming her thoughts about the man I once loved and was supposed to marry.

"Sky," I said, "Tom Tom was infected with HIV because of homosexual activity with another man and passed it on to me. Trina was the one he caught the virus from."

"How in the hell did he get the virus from Trina?" Sky looked confused. "Trina is a woman."

Sky slapped her hands over her mouth and started jumping up and down.

"Are you saying..?" she said. "What the..? Girl, I need a drink."

"I did, too," I said, "after Kendall told me she had a sex change."

"You mean Kendall knew all along," she said, "and didn't say anything about it? I say let's beat her, whatever's between its legs, and strangle the hoe."

"No, Sky," I said, "We cannot allow the flesh to overtake and make decisions that may hurt us later on."

Sky looked at me and shook her head.

"You a good one, honey," she said. "I will beat that thang until it's not recognized."

"You are just hateful, Sky," I said. "I am hurt. Yes, I am. But, Lord knows, I am not going to result to violence to please the flesh."

I looked down and rubbed my hands together.

"I have a lot to lose, retaliating," I said. "I may not like what a person does, but I will respect how I handle it."

"Well, do what your heart tells you, lady," Sky said, "because you asking the wrong person at the wrong time. And Kendall didn't say anything? Now that's some foul business!"

Temptations of the Flesh...

Twenty-five

I woke up early to a light, brisk autumn feel day. It was in the early 70's. A slight breeze chilled the air as I walked out on the patio for the morning air to awaken me more.

I noticed the leaves were confused about changing colors due to the unseasonable weather. I knew I was confused, too.

Christmas is coming up, I thought, *and ATL and I are still hanging in there. The ladies are still not pleased with our relationship, but whatever makes me happy, keeps them smiling.*

GOOD MORNING SUNSHINE.

It was ATL sending in an early morning text.

IS THE COFFEE BREWING?

YES, I texted back in haste.

What's going on? I wondered.

I rushed down the stairs to start a fresh brew. I didn't crank the pot on the weekends and ATL never came to see me on the weekends.

At this point, I only wanted to keep him around. "By any means necessary" was my plan to make him stick around a little while longer.

I boiled water for some grits, laced the cast iron skillet with some slow-cooking beef sausage patties, scrambled up some eggs and watched my red toaster pop the fresh bread by Sara Lee out the slots.

The entire house was filled with a hearty breakfast smell accompanied by the rich smell of the Arabian beans brewing ATL's taste buds straight into my arms.

"Good morning, lover," I soon said. We kissed one another passionately as the grits finished simmering, the cheese and me relaxing throughout.

"Good morning to you, lady," ATL said. "Ummm, you smell good, baby. And so does the food."

"Well, thank you, soldier," I said. "I smell you wearing the Usher cologne I got you. What gets you out the house on a weekend?"

"I picked up a few hours, but the couple that wanted some work done had a death in the family. So, here I am spending the entire Saturday with you. I got me a nice sack of weed, some blunts and a bottle of Courvoisier."

Temptations of the Flesh...

"Alright, lover," I said, "I'm smoking today and we are going to make whoopee all day long. Just as soon as you sit over here and get your belly full."

"You what..?" ATL said. "I have wanted to ask you pull off a little bit with me. I bet you are a freak when you high."

I grabbed ATL's hand and led him to the breakfast nook.

The energy we had for one another overtook the aroma of the coffee, grits, eggs, and toast. Passion began to steam up the bay window as our heavy panting and body heat sparked fire.

ATL grabbed me around my waist and slow danced while Anthony Hamilton's *Southern Stuff* played in the background.

My eyelids gyrated from the nibbling he gave my neck. Then he took his oversized hands and slowly rubbed them on the side of my face.

He cupped my head gently in his hands and kissed my glossy full lips. I reciprocated the passion by gentle rubbing the crease of his spine with my fingertips.

The breakfast table became our pallet. When ATL struggled to open the condom pack, I assisted his shaking hands to retrieve the rubber from the Life Style packaging.

Soon we were both weak in the knees and breathing out of control. Oxytocin stimulated our blood streams and caused the funk we shared.

"Damn, girl," ATL said, wiping sweat from my brow. "You were something else, lady."

"I know," I said. "Now get up and roll something so we can eat and get Round 2 started. We are going in all day."

I walked off giving him a seductive look.

ATL scurried off the table like a dog in heat and hurried to his favorite bathroom to shower and roll up.

I went to my bathroom and starting running a relaxing bath complete with bubbles, candles and a glass of Red Rose.

Soon I was interrupted by the smell of regular reefer stuffed in a Garcia Vega and ATL's fingers touching me as I bent over to check the temperature of the water.

"Round 2, huh?" I said.

I'm in control of this situation, I was thinking.

"Smoke," I dictated.

Breakfast for dinner is not a bad idea.

And, as I said, it was on all day.

Temptations of the Flesh...

Twenty-six

The phone rang and I looked at the caller ID. It was my mom.

"Hey, beautiful lady," I said. "How are you today?"

"I'm doing well, Gina," my mom said. "I hope you are. I had a dream last night and it didn't settle well with me. Is everything ok?"

When my mom calls about her dreams, I thought, *it means something is going to happen. Good or bad. And I am usually the person that it is going to happen to.*

"I'm okay, Mom," I said. "What about you?"

"I'm fine and dandy," she said. "I'm leaving in the morning to go to Chicago to visit your cousin and my sister. Aunt Flo isn't feeling well lately, so I'm going to fly out early in the morning and stay until Christmas Eve. I just want to make sure you are okay before I leave. If not, I will stay."

"No, Mom," I said. "Please go see about Auntie and keep me in prayer about an article I am writing as a contributor to Essence magazine."

I haven't even started it, I thought, *but it's been on my mind. The words I want to use, the opinions I want to give, are boldly ready to be confessed in written form.*

"There's not enough community awareness, not enough spotlight on HIV/AIDS as it is for cancer, Mom."

"Well, my dear," she said, "I will say a prayer as I always do for you and hope and pray it makes a difference as you continue to do so."

"Thanks, Mom," I smiled. "I send my love to Auntie. Have a safe trip."

I need to call and check on Ms. B, I thought.

Usually, I regularly checked in at the office, but due to my emotional displacement I hadn't talked to my assistant as much.

Just as I picked up the phone and began dialing I was interrupted by a phone message alert from Ms. B.

"Hey Ms. Regina," her cheery voice said, "I hope all is well. I just wanted to let you know all is well. You don't have any messages and I called everyone and explained your absence as you requested. Get plenty of rest. Remember to pray. Keep God first and see you after the New Year. Love ya."

It feels so good to have a caring and compassionate personal assistant like Ms. B, I thought. I called her and simply said Thank You, ordered some flowers and a massage, giving her the rest of the month off with pay.

ATL arrived at my place without a text or a phone call.

His comfort level is stable, I thought, *because he knows he has me where he needs me to be.*

"Hey, sweet thang," he said, "let's go lay down in the bed for a while. I miss holding you."

"I miss holding you, too," I said.

I stopped by the ET room and put on my favorite CD, the one ATL made for me. I started it on my favorite song, Track 6, *Last First Kiss.*

As we walked slowly up the stairs, ATL stopped and turned to me.

"Regina," he said, "how do you feel about getting married?"

"I don't know," I lied, "I never thought about it after the last time I was supposed to get married."

"So, you were asked before?" he said.

"Yes," I said.

Doesn't he remember what I told him when we first met? I don't want to go into the details with ATL about Tom Tom, I thought. *It's already embarrassing enough what my friends think. I don't need the man I'm kicking it with to know I got caught slipping on what kind of man I had.*

As we made our way to my bedroom, I laid across the bed. ATL was on the other side and continued to ramble off about getting married.

This excited me to a minimum.

I don't want to get my hopes up too high, I thought, *but, at the same time, it is pleasant to be wanted again.*

"What colors would you want, Gina?" ATL said.

I looked at him and didn't see anything in his hands.

"What are you talking about?" I said.

"Our wedding colors." he said.

"Are you serious?" I said.

"Yes," he said, "I want to know what colors you want in our wedding."

I giggled.

I don't know if he is playing with my head or truly expressing a "happily ever after," I thought.

"Red and white," I said. "I love the color red—it's Love--the blood of Jesus--and it's a beautiful color. White is as pure as you get when it comes to matching up the perfect colors for a wedding. That's the color I always wanted since I was a little girl. What about you?"

"It's whatever you want, Regina. I want to be with you. I just need you to give me a little more time. She has been tripping lately. You know she took my check and thought she lost it. I found it, and was like, me and you can go off and do some shopping. She can be stuck with that house note."

I looked sideways at ATL. That *"She"* again.

"You think I'm stupid or something, man?" I said.

"No, baby, I don't think you're stupid. You are a beautiful woman and I want to spend the rest of my life with you. But in another 10 days it will be Christmas. I want to see my baby girl's First Christmas, Regina. You have to understand that."

I looked at him with my heart instead of my head.

My heart is melting, I thought, *just as it did in the beginning--but, this time, my stomach is empty.*

Soon Marriage became the topic of discussion for us. Ms. Thing was illuminated so radiantly I bounced positive energy onto everyone I made contact with. My friends told me I was glowing from head to toe. Even my shoes looked like they were spit-shined...

Twenty-seven

As Christmas grew closer, my light of hope was dimming and the days grew shorter. The nights didn't move along well with the moon, either.

"ATL," I said one day, "your days are shorter than your nights with me. You keep talking about you want to get married...and give you some time with the same breath. The baby's First Christmas and all this. Come on, man. What are you going to do to keep me happy during the holidays? How do I know you are not sure what you want to do? I don't want a repeat performance of Thanksgiving. I don't want a repeat performance of my first proposal for a marriage that didn't happen."

It's time for me to see how things are popping off for ATL, I thought. *This baby has a strong hold on this man and I understand that to a certain degree. I don't have any children, so it's confusing to me.*

The next night I decided to put on some sweat and a Hoodie and headed to the garage. This time I pulled out my custom-painted Mercedes Benz--dark blue with peanut butter interior, a five-speed with all the accessories, enough to make a passenger wish the key ring was in their pocket.

I palmed my BlackBerry Curve in my hand and flipped through the applications to get the GPS address I had left in the Maps.

The time is right, I thought. *Tonight is the night to see how Mr. ATL is living. Maybe I can catch a glance at old girl…not to make my presence known…just to see what he is working with.*

Temptations of the Flesh…

I was only hoping to catch a glance at old girl, not to make my presence known, just to see what he was working with.

I slowly pulled up to the three-story brick home with a freshly cut lawn and manicured trees…with an oil spot in the driveway.

The same spots stain my driveway, I thought. *And now I make him park on the street.*

A large bay window sat with tied curtains and sheers draped down the middle hosting the beauty of a Douglas Fir Christmas tree glistening with white lights.

More light gleamed from what appeared to be the kitchen or dining area. The large opening allowed me to see large palm trees that accentuated the living area.

I drove slowly and repeatedly, passing the immaculate living arrangements,

"Hmmm," I said aloud, "Either she has a good job or ATL is installing satellites all over the country."

I had seen enough and decided to head back to my own home, less than four minutes away.

They say accidents happen close to home.

Temptations of the Flesh…

Twenty-eight

It was time for me to get on the ball with my Christmas shopping--shopping especially for the best friends a girl could ever hope for.

I had no idea what to get Trina. I still had a heart of gold and didn't hold anything against her for what had happened. I accepted responsibility. And tried to move forward. This would be her first Christmas in Charlotte and I was doing an early Christmas gathering because the ladies opted to have Christmas in Miami this year.

I felt it was only right to stay in Charlotte since it would be my first Christmas with ATL. I was praying for a different outcome than the one I had for Thanksgiving.

Things seemed to be blending pretty well for me lately. I knew my prayer life suffered a lot and my focus was taking a detour. I knew having another person's presence in my life was keeping me from mastering the skill of perfecting God's purpose for me on earth. I knew that strengthening my relationship with God was the one that really mattered.

GOOD MORNING DARK AND LOVELY.

I read the text ATL sent.

GOOD MORNING TO YOU HANDSOME, I texted back.

IM ON MY WAY, he replied.

I was not used to seeing ATL on a Saturday morning. But I loved it when he could switch his jobs around and make me feel important.

Saturday morning coffee will not be the same.

However, ATL came with a visitor with him this time.

He was dressed in street clothes and armed with a diaper bag and a plump-sized bundle wrapped in a pink blanket.

"Good morning," he said as he rushed through the door."

I couldn't blame him. The weather had started to feel like winter wanted to invade the autumn brisk--just in time, five days before Christmas.

"Shawty," he said, "this is my daughter Ariel."

Ariel rubbed her eyes and lifted her large head off her daddy's chest. She turned her big marble-brown eyes in my direction.

She studied me closely and looked around at the unfamiliar surroundings and extended her arms towards me.

I stood stunned and in awe of a baby I had never met whose spirit was mixing with mine.

"I don't know anything about any babies, man," I said to ATL, trying to laugh this experience off.

I do not want to hold this baby. Oh no.

"Go ahead, Regina," ATL said, "she won't bite." He began to laugh at me as I reached out with hesitation and transferred Ariel from his arms to mine.

She began to rub her soft chubby hands on my chin and pressed her index finger on my curvy Red Cherry lashes.

I tried to hand her back to him, but his hand went up signaling his need for me to watch her while he made a quick run.

I stood before him with the baby in my arms, but the expression on my face said, "What am I supposed to do and how long you are going to be gone?"

This is not right, I was thinking. *I don't feel a connection here. ATL knows my feelings are lop-sided for him. He's using any means necessary to make me into the desperate woman he first met, a woman desperate for a man...and a family.*

"Hurry back," I said instead.

Twenty-nine

Four days before Christmas

I finally let my friends that didn't know in on the deal with the Tom Tom and Trina scandal. They all had questions. Some questions I could answer and some I had to find out about in a letter that came to me in the mail from Dallas, Texas. It was addressed Priority Mail.

I opened it.

The letter was from Trina's case manager in Dallas.

What in the world is Trina's case manager doing sending me a letter?

I began to read. Soon I was grabbing my shirt as tears streamed from my eyes.

Dear Regina BoRose,

I regret to inform you of the passing of your dear friend, Trina Brown, on December 18. She suffered a massive heart attack..."

I sat down in the middle of the floor and began to cry uncontrollably

"Father God." I screamed out. "In the Precious Name of Jesus, thank You for saving me."

Trina had put me down as an emergency contact just in case something happened.

And it had.

Three days before Christmas

I flew to Dallas for Trina's funeral and even had the opportunity to visit the grave site where Tom was buried to get some things off my chest, things I needed to say to his lying spirit and dishonest dust.

I left my anger there in Texas. Although not many people showed up, Trina was put away nicely.

The kid she had—who birth circumstances I never understood after all that Kendall had told me--I later found out was her younger adopted brother. Trina had taken him in after her mom passed away from cancer.

Two days before Christmas

Christmas was happening right here in my own home. The smell of cinnamon filled the air. I picked the perfect night to wrap gifts. The house was clear of everyone.

I knew I was still delicate, still in a state of trying to figure out who I was.

"It's Me time," I said to myself. After all the sad activity, this was the first time I had been alone in a while and it felt good.

No music was playing. The quiet of the night suppressed anything that tried to get in the way of the calmness I felt. But I felt a tugging at my arm as if someone was pulling me.

I began to get on my knees to stand up, but I found myself paralyzed in the position, on my knees.

I began to cry, suddenly understanding God was charging me to pray.

"Father," I yelled out, "I need you right now! You have spared my life so many times and kept me from hurt, harm and danger. Thank you, Lord, in the Name of Your Precious Son, Jesus. I come to you with a heavy heart."

I had no idea from where all this faith, emotion, and fervency came. It seemed like I was turning into another person, the woman God needed me to be, submissive to His will, in His presence and needing Him and no one else.

My heart began to get heavy inside of me as I poured out my desires to Him.

"Lord, forgive me for being so needy," I confessed. "Forgive me for being against your will and fornicating with this man.

"This man," I screamed, "who makes me smile, Lord. ATL makes me smile. So, keep me in your arms, Lord. Forgive me for putting someone before you. You are truly the One who will make me smile for eternity."

Spit, tears and mucous smeared my face as I lay down on the chocolate-brown carpet in my room. I slept till the morning sun caressed my face.

I was surprised at no morning text to remind me to unlock the door or even a good morning from ATL.

What is going on?

I dialed his number, feeling a certain kind of way--you know, that feeling you feel when you have been stood up or rejected.

His phone was disconnected.

Thirty

Two days before Christmas

"Good morning, lady, it's been a long time since we seen you in the shop." It was Annta, a friend I rarely got to see but when we got together we had a wonderful time laughing and catching up.

"Yes," I said, "I had to get some things in order."

"Look at TC with his no-talking self," I shouted out.

"What's up, mama," TC called back, "you looking like Ms. Gladys today."

TC always has something crazy to say to me. This brother has a beautiful voice. I call him the Velvet Teddy Bear. He takes off where Gerald Levert left off. He can't speak a sentence without adding extra syllables, but his voice will melt your heart. He's a heavy set R&B crooner and makes everyone wonder why he hasn't hit it big yet with a CD.

"I'm the big boy from the group home," he was saying. His laugh was so jolly.

Just what I need this Christmas laughter.

It was good to be back in the shop.

When Kendall came in, I couldn't bring myself to say a word to him. I missed him, yet I was still hurt he had kept the secret about Tom Tom for so long. He could have saved me the agony of the experience.

"Come on, lady," Tiny shouted out, "let me get in that bird's nest of yours."

I sprung up from my seat to avoid making any eye contact with Kendall and proceeded to get my hair done in silence.

Tiny didn't bother me much. She knew I was still upset about everything that had transpired. ATL still hadn't made contact with me and it was burning me up.

I decided to make a run over to his house while my hair was molded and semi-dry.

Just one more ride, I thought, *just to scope things out. How could that hurt?*

Temptations of the Flesh...

Thirty-one

Christmas Eve Day

Today is a new day, I thought upon waking, *a new day to make it right. No phone calls from Ms. B. No one is asking for my appearance to speak at events.*

What is going on?

Here I am stuck on stupid with a man that is spoken for. My donations are down in the third quarter.

My Range Rover is acting crazy. Every week for about a month it's been in and out the shop.

Something was out of order and I knew it was me.

Man, this flesh of mine is weak.

I had tossed and turned all night after my experiences at ATL's house the day before.

The whole rest of that day didn't go right and I didn't even return for Tiny to finish my hair.

Sad as it may sound, I began wishing I had stayed with Blue, the demon I knew.

After seeing the Christmas tree lit up and cars parked in front of

ATL's home, I had finally realized the battle was within me. Inwardly, it was I who was DESPERATE for love. And my desperation had taken me in the wrong direction.

After getting out of bed I decided I would hang out at the shop to keep my mind off of things. The shop was group therapy for me and today was a good day to seek some humorous counseling.

"What it do, everybody?" I shouted out in the crowded shop.

"What's up, you Chubby Chaser?" Big Game shouted out. Big Game is a tall slender pecan- brown barber who has a soul as old as Jerusalem.

"What do you mean 'Chubby Chaser'?" I asked him, feeling a bit defensive.

"You know what I'm talking about, Gina."

Big Game, also known as the Granddaddy in the shop, motioned with his head for me to come towards him.

"You have too much going on for you to be chasing someone you see bigger than what God has before you," he whispered.

Tears formed in my eyes because the statement cut like a knife. I was embarrassed to know anyone knew I was stalking this man.

"How did you know?" I asked.

"Eyes are watching, girl," he said. "You have a legacy to fulfill. Be patient and wait on yours. Don't settle."

He winked at me and pushed me gently out of his way.

"Get on, you Chubby Chaser," he said. "Do the right thang."

I secretly wiped my tears and went in the bathroom to wash my face.

"*Father*," I said, "*can You hear me?*"

I turned the water up and the fan on in the bathroom so no one would interrupt my time with God.

"*I know You must be tired of me coming to You in this way over and over again for the same thing, getting the same results.*

"*When is it my turn? Why do I fall for temptation? What is it that allows me to not resist this man or any other man?*

"*Over and over I ask You the same questions. I pray and repent. You forgive and I turn right around and do it all over again.*

"*And the saddest part is I don't wait on Your answer, Your confirmation, Your revelation, Your plan for me.*"

"**Be still, my child. Be still.**" God answered.

Thirty-two

Christmas Day

The birds were chirping "Good Morning" and "Merry Christmas," but my BlackBerry still hadn't alerted me with a text from ATL.

"What, in the Name of Jesus, is going on?" I said out loud.

I want some closure. Plus, I got this dude a Christmas gift and I most definitely want what he has for me. I think.

The night before I had enjoyed a magnificent night with the ladies before they boarded their plane to Miami for the holidays. I could have still gone, but I couldn't bring myself to be gone through Christmas.

Now I kind of wish I had. **Choices.**

After calling the ladies and wishing them a Merry Christmas I went towards the bathroom to take a quick shower and was stopped as a peace came upon me.

I was planning to run water in the tub when I was interrupted by a text message.

MERRY CHRISTMAS BABY OPEN THE DOOR.

ATL has come to rescue my emotions, I thought.

I quickly forgot about my dying soul and submerging myself in the tub of water. Instead, I opted to open the door.

Temptations of the Flesh...
No one was there.

I looked down at the ground. There, in front of the door, lay a small red envelope--and nothing else.

"No box with the DeAngelo William's jersey?" I spoke to the wind.

I really wanted that jersey.

Once inside the house, I found a small card was in the envelope--a card with no signature--and a gift card to The Olive Garden for $25.00.

"You got to be kidding me?" I said to myself.

This is a joke.

I looked at my BlackBerry and saw ATL had sent another message,

SORRY I COULDNT GET YOU WHAT YOU ASKED FOR THE JERSEYS WERE SOLD OUT BUT HAVE YOU ONE ON LAY A WAY.

"Are you serious?"

Fire was coming out of every opening of my body and the steam caused a combustion that ejected my BlackBerry across the room.

Temptations of the Flesh...
This man has lost his everlasting mind. He has tried me for real this time. I can't do anything but laugh this off.

But I decided to get back where it hurt. I sent him a text.

BROTHER YOU HAVE CROSSED THE WRONG ONE. YOU HAVE SOME NERVE TO BRING ME SOMETHING YOU PROBABLY GOT FROM YOUR JOB'S CHRISTMAS PARTY.

But, I wasn't ready to push Send yet.

Fuming smoke was clouding my thinking and my next move was devastating. Everything I had been praying on my knees for was viciously captivated by the powers of my flesh.

I added the very words hated most by men from the woman they are creeping with.

I'M GOING TO TELL YOUR WOMAN EVERYTHING!

I pushed the Send button.

It wasn't five minutes and he was at my door in her car, a black Lexus.

"Gina, baby," he pleaded from the other side of the door, "please, don't do this to me. Please, let's talk it out."

I became the African-American Sybil.

"Nah, man," I said, "you have some nerve to not only text me to open the door but use a lame tactic to leave this weak gift on my doorstep."

I swung the door open with force, the beginning of tears in my eyes and a baseball bat in my hand.

"All we have been through," I screamed, "and all I was worth was a dinner for one at Olive Garden?"

"Red Lobster and Fridays are an option also," he said sarcastically.

I picked the unsigned card up and smashed it in his face. The bat was swinging close.

"What in the world do you get off giving me a card that you couldn't even sign?" I said. "If you couldn't handle the pressure you shouldn't have played me to play with your pipes."

I paced back and forth in front of the door, every inch of me holding back tears and laughing at the same time. My multiple personalities were dipping in and out of the argument with the Louisville slugger in my hand.

"I can't believe I lay with you," I cried. "You are weak. You are a poor excuse for a man. I am no better, but you will not try me like this. I deserve better. You couldn't spend $200.00 on me for Christmas? And whose car are you driving?"

"That's my Baby Mama car," he said.

"You drove her car to my house and parked it in my driveway?" I hollered back. "You got some nerve. I ought to bust out every window in that Lexus!"

I was screaming at the top of my lungs. I charged towards the open door as ATL dropped to his knees with tears in his eyes.

"I'm sorry, Gina," he said. "Please. I need to confess something."

"What is it?" I screamed. "Everything you say is a lie. How can I trust you?"

"Gina. Please, listen to me. I'm on the run, baby. Please."

He grabbed me by my hand and tried to grab hold of the bat.

"Please, pray with me," he said. "Please, Gina, you know how to pray. Show me how to pray."

I was stunned. His words stopped me cold and brought me out of my rage.

"Seriously..?" I asked. "You don't know how to pray?"

"Gina," he said, "nobody has ever showed me how to pray. Please."

ATL got on his knees with whitened lips and tears in his eyes, shaking like a leaf on a tree.

I couldn't say a thing.

He jumped up.

"I will do it myself," he said.

You were taught to pray with someone who asks. I can't have it on my conscience to not obey his request. No matter how mad I am at him.

I grabbed ATL by his hands and started to pray: *"Our Father Who art in Heaven, Hallowed be Thy name... Thy Kingdom come... Thy will be done on Earth as it is in Heaven... Give us this day our daily bread... Forgive us our sins, as we forgive those who sin against us. Lead us not into temptation, but deliver us from evil... For Thine is the Kingdom, the Power and the Glory... Forever and ever. Amen."*

I completed The Lord's Prayer with tears in my eyes.

Afterwards ATL told me about the charge he had been running from in the A. It was a murder case, he said, and it had resurfaced.

"Atlanta detectives are looking for me," he concluded. "I don't want to impose my life style on you or ruin your reputation with a past conviction coming back to haunt me."

I still wasn't satisfied.

Somebody is going to pay for this hurt and pain you caused me.

I smiled at him as a plan formed in my mind.

Vengeance is mine, I thought, totally ignoring God's Word that tells me Vengeance is His to bestow.

Temptations of the Flesh...

Thirty-three

The day after Christmas

Today was another new day all over again.

Second chances, a trillion times.

But God kept waking me up to the nightmare this life of mine had become.

It's not that I'm not thankful, Lord, but I need to do better in walking the way You have destined for me. I need to make the best of it and get my whole life together.

I missed the ladies' empowerment groups and couldn't wait for the New Year to get back into the swing of things.

These ladies need me, I thought. *And truth be told, I need them.*

But, I had some unfinished business to tend to.

I grabbed a pen and some paper and started writing my Dear John Letter to ATL's woman.

Four pages later of the When, Why, How and Where the letter was delivered—her home being only four minutes and seven seconds away.

It was signed, sealed and delivered:

Lady Libra, the truth on your lying-behind man…
Temptations of the Flesh…
Three days before the New Year.

"Good morning, Regina, we have the estimate on your Range Rover."

Shorty was my mechanic at the Havoline Fast Lube on Brookshire Blvd. and was sure to break even on the repairs.

"Good morning, Shorty," I said, "what's the deal with it now?"

"Well, for starters," he said, "your water pump is busted. It needs to be replaced and your radiator has a crack in it. We need to replace that as well. You are due for an inspection and you need to get your oil change, too, Ms. Gina-Gina…"

I sighed with a shake of my head.

"How much?" I said bluntly.

"Well, baby girl," he said, "you know the routine. Either you get the parts and pay for the labor or allow us to do it and bust out a credit card and charge $978.00 to it."

"I need that truck fixed," I said.

Even though I had multiple cars this car was specifically for business.

"OK," I said. "Go ahead. I don't have time to get anything, so just do what you do and call me when it's ready."

I had spent close to $2500 on this truck in the past month and it wasn't looking like the problems were going to let up.

Then that Gentle Voice pierced me in my side saying, *"I blessed you with this car to do My purpose not to make a fool out of you."*

I stood still and a spirit of humility came upon me. I realized I needed to ask Shorty for forgiveness and apologize for my rudeness.

It seems my flesh constantly fights back and forth with the Holy Spirit, I thought, *and a hard shell encloses my heart—and its beat is irregular. Boldly I confess my sins over and over again to You, Lord, asking for forgiveness--only to feel unsaved all over again.*

Time seemed to be ticking audibly as I tried to wait patiently on ATL to show his face or, at least, call. I was bracing myself for his reaction to what I had done. It would be soon. I felt the least he could do was to hear me out.

I had left the four page letter in his mailbox. I also knew he had gone to work when I left it there because I saw him drive off in his company van.

"Good morning, sunshine, what's going on with you?" It was Holiday calling from Florida.

"I'm good," I said. "What's the deal with you girls? How is South Beach?"

"Everything is everything, girl," she said. "We wish you would have come down with us."

"I know," I murmured.

"Excuse me?" Holiday said, laughing. "What did I hear you say? What has happened, Gina-girl? Did ATL hit you with another Thanksgiving repeat?"

"He might   as well have," I said. "You know this clown had the nerve to get--"

I didn't get the words out my mouth before my line clicked.

I looked at the caller ID. It was ATL.

"Hold on Holiday... Hello," I said to ATL.

"Gina," he said, "how could you? How could you do this to me? You tore my family apart. I told you to just wait on me. Wait until after Christmas, so I could see my baby girl's First Christmas."

ATL was truly angry. I heard an unfamiliar tone that had never surfaced before in our relationship.

"You have to understand my position as a woman here," I said. "You made a lot of promises to me and didn't follow through. You slacked up on coming to see me. You lied to me on Thanksgiving and were a No Show.

"You spoke hot air about getting married, wanting to marry me. You changed your mind on my gift you asked me about for Christmas.

And then you had the nerve to text me to open the door and left me an envelope with a gift card that was probably given to you from your job. Dude, who do you think you're dealing with?"

ATL's silence from the other end just made me a little hotter. I began to feel that piercing in my side again, reminding who I needed to be in this situation.

A quick glimpse into my Fears and my Future came from the spiritual realm and began to unfold before me.

Fear #1: My speaking engagements are down.

The Future: I could see a room filled with people and me standing before them.

Fear #2: My donations are down.

The Future: A glance at my check book and ledger revealed the rewards for the times I was in His will and not standing in the way of His blessings.

Get yourself together, girl, I thought. *Your spirit is crushed and you haven't been in the mood to go to church or praise God as you should, and yet, you stand here arguing with a man that has no substance.*

Fear #3: Losing ATL.

The Future: A shadow of a man appeared with no face. He was calmly walking away.

I am not ready for any man, I realized quickly. *I have been giving my power over to someone that has no relevance, no position or purpose for my life. I can go on and on....*

"Stop it now!" A voice of reason came upon me. "STOP IT NOW!"

"Okay, ATL," I was able to say. "Before I go to my Father in Heaven for forgiveness I must ask you for forgiveness. I apologize for doing all that I have done to cause confusion, including getting involved with you in the first place, fornicating, lusting and doing things we had no business doing.

"The Bible tells me in the book of Matthew 6:14-16 that if I forgive those who sin against me, my heavenly Father will forgive me. But, if I refuse to forgive others, My Father will not forgive me."

"I hear what you are saying, Gina," he said. "I accept your apology. I honestly can say that, but to forgive you--I can't do that."

I was actually shocked that he had given me at least an inch. I knew this was the end of ATL and me, but I had to make it known. I had to speak.

"ATL," I said, "I appreciate you accepting my apology and I understand you fully. Now I also understand the reasons for our relationship which should have been simply a friendship. I crossed the line when I imposed my fleshly desires upon you.

"I now know I was put here to simply show you how to pray. I took advantage of my freedom and liberty in God to sin. I didn't recognize it for as long as I did because my flesh dominated what was not being fed—and what was not being fed was my spiritual side."

What are these words? I marveled. *Where are they coming from?*

I could feel a newness quickly forming within me. I was visually impaired from the tears in my eyes. My heart rhythm began to beat more peacefully, in a pattern that was no longer subject to irregularity.

This miracle was happening just in time. My Daddy had stepped in. I knew I was being saved by Mercy.

"ATL," I said, "it's fine. You don't have to forgive me right now, but do it sooner rather than later. You do not have to let me know verbally, but let our Father in Heaven know.

"I will send up a prayer of Thanksgiving beforehand acknowledging the time in the future when you will forgive me. I accept it in truth.

"Again, babe, I am apologizing for my weakness, for my immaturity. Our relationship was not meant to be the way it was. I allowed the satisfaction of my flesh to come first and ignored your need for Him. I was simply meant to teach you how to pray.

"Goodbye, ATL, and blessings to you."

Dying Flesh…

Thirty-four

The night before New Year's Eve

I got a call from the ladies that their plane had landed and it was off to the airport to pick up my girls.

I pulled up to the arrival lot and they all were standing there with MIA shirts, big mugs and leis around their necks.

I shook my head at the humor my girls displayed and the happiness they were having on the walkway of Charlotte Douglas International

Airport. Holiday, Sky, Jade, and Tiny, were back on North Carolina grounds.

I made up in my mind to immediately get off my chest the mess that had transpired while they were away. I needed to tell them how I had righted my wrongs and held on in spite of the foolishness I had caused.

"I can't believe you stooped so low to write his woman an Aaliyah letter," Sky shouted when I was finished. "You are a woman of minimum mistakes and this one is the ultimate low self-esteem mistake of them all. I love you, girl, but a true sister is not going to condone your actions. We are here to love you unconditionally—but, at the same time, when you are wrong you are wrong."

"Yeah, Gina," Tiny said. "Sky is right. I am not here to judge you or pick a wound that seems to be healing, but, baby girl, this can't happen again. This type of behavior is not allowed. How do you expect God to bless you with a man acting like this?"

"Tiny is right, too," Holiday said. "Look at what you almost lost: your reputation. You sat down on your True Passion for a passion that was weakening you."

I looked over at Holiday talking to me with tears in her eyes.

"I never want you to go through what I have been through," she continued, "married to a man that I'm not in love with, searching for others to keep me content and sneaking in the process, all while breaking my covenant with God."

"You have been through so much, Gina," Jade said. "The diagnosis almost took you out. Then you found out Tom was gay. Then he marries a transgender who befriended you. She dies and, meanwhile, your best buddy knew all along and he didn't say anything--not a word, and just a slip of the tongue could have saved your from all of this."

"*Temptations of the Flesh* live with us all, dear friends," I said. "They live with us all."

The car was silent all the way home.

Before I dropped each one off, I asked them to attend the Watch Night Service with me at church for New Year's Eve.

They all agreed.

Good friends are hard to find, keep, and keep it real. Thank you, Lord, for my Faithful Four.

Thirty-five

New Year's Eve

Watch Night 2009 was the perfect time to go back in the house of the Lord without shame and with boldness. Plus, it was needed.

I was tired of holding back the pressure and I needed to make amends with God.

Holiday, Jade, Sky and Tiny all made the service at the small nondenominational church I attend. We would fellowship in spirit and in truth.

The Praise and Worship Team filled the air with beautiful songs glorifying His name and ushering in His presence.

"If anyone in the House of the Lord died right now," the Pastor asked, "would you be confident where your soul would rest?"

I was uneasy and nervous yet felt this question was for me. If I didn't get up now I might not have another chance.

Then, suddenly, Sky got up and walked down the steps to the altar to give her life to Christ. Glory Hallelujah!

We were ringing with happiness and all had tears in our eyes.

Then Holiday walked up and did the same.

This was a profound moment for me—and it didn't stop there.

The Pastor who was preaching this night was a woman that I had never heard of before. The Lord was using her to speak directly to my spirit.

Before the service I had made up in my mind to keep it a one-on-one conversation with God after I got home--but it was coming sooner than I anticipated.

"I am talking to the backslider," she was saying, "who has a Promise for her life and a Destiny waiting to unfold...yet, because of temptations to please her own flesh knows she is falling short... NOW is your time to come back.

"To the woman or the man who has lost his or her way because of battle with the mind...NOW is your time to come back."

The pastor stood with arms stretched out towards the congregation.

"To the Child of God who once stood on the battlefield for the Lord," she said, "but feels defeated due to finances, a broken heart, or, perhaps, you are just lost in the world, feeling all alone. Will you come? Come and rededicate yourself back to God."

The choir began to sing an old gospel hymn, *Pass Me Not, Old Gentle Savior...*

When the words got to the second verse, I began to feel another piercing in my side.

> *Let me at a throne of Mercy*
> *Find a sweet relief;*
> Kneeling there in deep contrition,
> *Help my unbelief.*

These were the words that made me stand up. I wanted to be at that altar.

With tears streaming down my face, I floated from the balcony to the main floor of the sanctuary of the packed out church. I was ready to say my vows as the Psalmist, King David, said, "in the midst of the congregation."

All I could see myself doing was to present myself to God, face down at the altar, with my arms spread apart, crying my heart out to Him.

Father, please forgive me. You know my situation. You know my faults. You are the Only One that can right my wrongs. I need Your forgiveness.

For the first time in my life I felt free. Free to love on God, free to love on me and free of all that had me in bondage.

Thirty-six

The New Year

Tiny asked me if I would assist her at the shop before I went back to work.

As I waited one morning for the day's work to begin, I received a message on my BlackBerry from Ms. Brandee:

GOOD MORNING MS. G. YOU HAVE A REQUESTS FOR YOUR APPEARANCE IN NEW ORLEANS, NEW YORK, AND GREENVILLE, NC. PLEASE CHECK YOUR EMAIL.

Tears streamed down my face. Favor was finally showing its beautiful head my way again.

I worked in the shop through the weekend and finally got enough nerve to go up to Kendall and ask him if we could talk.

"I miss you, buddy," I said.

"I miss you, too, big head," he said. "I am sorry for keeping that from you, Gina, baby. I didn't have a reason not to and, as close as we are, I owe you. I know I can't take back what has been done, but I can mean it from my heart to never defy you again."

I grabbed my little big brother and hugged him tight.

"I love you, Kendall. I miss you, too. You owe me nothing, man, just come back into my life as we used to be. But you have to promise one thing,"

"What's that, Gina, baby, anything for you?"

I looked at him with a smile.

"Church on Sunday" I said.

"Okay," he said, "Church on Sunday."

Things were finally getting back to normal for me. My aunt was doing a lot better and the nagging from my mom about having a man and getting married had ceased. Believe it or not, that helped submerge the temptations a lot. I didn't feel I had to accomplish anything I was not meant to pursue in the first place.

I went back to Grace Memorial and began doing the weekly workshops with HIV Positive women at Girls in the Hood. I also picked up some Park and Recreational groups and church ministries for single women struggling with low self- esteem.

From time to time I still wondered what had become of ATL. I was not being tempted but felt a valid and genuine concern to know what had happened to him, especially if he was continuing to pray.

I decided to call Kendall and ask.

"Man," Kendall said, "ATL is not doing too good. He lost his job. Real talk, Gina, baby…he thinks you had something to do with it."

"Seriously..?" I said. "I promise you I had nothing to do with that. What happened?"

"Well," he said, "ATL was out installing satellites and the big boss came out on site and told him to come down off the ladder. Then they took him to get a random urinalysis."

"Wow!" I said, "I promise you, Kendall, I didn't do that. I admitted to ATL what I did and can talk about that, but this right here, what you are talking about now, was not me."

I immediately felt sorry for ATL, but had to realize I could not let myself interfere with God and His work in ATL's life.

I remembered what God had me tell ATL about forgiving others so that we could be forgiven.

"I told him that didn't sound like you right there," Kendall was saying. "Now that other stuff was a woman scorned--this right here was dead wrong on his part because he knew his job could pop up anytime and test him."

"Well," I said," if you see him, let him know that wasn't me."

I hated that this was the way things ended, but God has a way of showing me to get out of the way just in time. I never should have been there in the first place, but in order to learn from a temptation you have to be tempted.

I decided on my outfit for the speaking engagement in New Orleans and packed all my stuff for the four day/three night event.

Then it was time to get to the shop and get my hair done.

As it had been months since ATL had even crossed my mind, this day was destined to be a day I would never forget.

"Hey, Gina, what's good, lady?" Tiny greeted me.

"I'm great, girl," I said, "getting ready to catch this US AIR to New Orleans--so get me right so I can get to the airport on time."

Tiny immediately washed and molded me down and sat me under the dryer. Under the heat, I began to nod off to sleep. Suddenly I felt a shadow standing over me and opened my eyes.

"ATL," I said, startled by his presence. "How are you?"

"I'm fine, Gina," he said. "May I sit down?"

He removed the dryer from over my head.

"Sure," I said, positioning myself for the unexpected.

"Remember when you told me to forgive and be forgiven?"

"Yes," I replied.

"Well, Gina, please know I forgive you. I actually forgave you a long time ago. I will never forget, though," ATL chuckled. "But I will never go through life not realizing what I learned from this."

I looked at him.

"What was that?" I said.

"Well, for starters, keep it real with all women, especially a woman like you. Never go outside the relationship. And never leave a woman in your car with an unlocked glove compartment."

We both laughed.

"Well," I said, "how are things with you and your girl?"

"We are still not there, man," he said. "You told her everything."

"That's over and done with," I interrupted.

"Yeah, it is," he said. "I want you to know I prayed to God and told Him I forgave you and things started to change for me. I went back to school. I own a tractor trailer now, shipping cargo across country, making good money."

"God is good," I said.

"Thank you, Gina," he said and kissed me on my hand. "This ordeal made me a better man."

I left the shop feeling refreshed. Not because of the hairdo or the trip to New Orleans, but because I had stepped aside.

On my way back from New Orleans I reminisced on the African-American Women's Summit I had attended. I realized I had learned a lot about myself and what God expected of me as a woman--and it didn't include chasing a man.

I had done the unthinkable trying to keep a man. I had most definitely disrespected myself trying to get back at one man because of my self-inflicted wounds. I was the one who had caused more problems than anyone else.

Once home, I dropped my bags and thumbed through my mail. One letter that didn't surprise me was from Blue—return address: the Mecklenburg County Jail. I put it in the trash.

I hurried upstairs to my secret closet, my bathroom, and ran some water to pray and meditate on the Glory of God and the Almighty Goodness He was bringing into my life. I poured in the milk, honey, and lavender mix and fell to my knees beside the garden tub.

A song of praise came from my lips.

"Thank You, Lord, for finding me in time. I thank You for safe travels and allowing me to just say Thank You one more time. You have been so good to me, more than I could ever be to myself.

"I know I am not perfect, Lord, and I ask You to take full control of me. I give my heart to You, Lord, make it new. I give my body to You Lord, cleanse me."

I stood up and removed my clothing, reached in my purse and took out the bottle of Olive Oil I had gotten from the store--a bottle I had yet to pray over and anoint myself with.

As I prayed over the oil, I asked God to bless it and make it Holy.

Like Esther, in preparation to be the Queen, I would bathe in oil. I wiped it, first, across my forehead and asked for the renewing of my mind.

I wiped it over my eyes and asked to be protected from evil...
My ears I saturated so that I might be careful to hear things that are
pleasing to my Creator...I wiped my nose and asked God to keep a
sweet smell in the air...I greased my lips and asked for protection over
what I say...I touched my body parts and asked Him for continued
healing...I reached down to my belly button.

"Lord," I said in a loud voice, "please numb me from the belly
button down. Allow me this, Lord, until you are ready for me to be
with the man that is my husband."

I stepped into the warm bath and blessed the prayer with an Amen.
I washed my sorrows away and watched as the debris drained out.

I sat bare-naked and shouted unto God with the Praise of
Victory.

Epilogue

I was seated for lunch at the Chipotle Mexican Grill in the south end of Charlotte. I had just pushed Send to my Editor for this manuscript of *My Last First Kiss*.

I sighed in relief because I had done what God asked me to do.

I have to admit I am built from a different cloth: I will admit things many will not. I will confess things many won't dare share. I know the reason why--I want to help someone else that is going through the same things I have overcome. At least, in this situation, anyway, I daily shed dead skin.

I've learned to walk with authority. I've learned to stay focused on God and maintain a presence in Him.

I know God has called me to do extraordinary works with women and girls. He has left me here for that reason.

The ultimate goal is for those who meet me to see God in me. I know my goal in life is to help those who don't have an intimate relationship with God develop one--and go on to live life in Spirit and in Truth.

I can no longer do the things of the world that are not pleasing to God. I can no longer go out in the world and speak of His goodness and be hypocritical in the process.

I thank God for this. God is who He is and not like man.

To my ladies who are loving impurely: STOP IT. It's not fair to you or to the God in you to walk around putting stipulations and conditions on a relationship that is not meant to be.

I was simply not ready for marriage or a man, for that matter. Nor was marriage or a man ready or willing for me. God is not going to bless us accordingly until we line up with what is expected of us.

How dare we say "I'm ready, Lord," and we haven't even thrown away love letters and pictures of men who still have a special place in our hearts, yet they belong to another?

How dare we save emails and text messages in our phones from someone that has no substance or relevance in our lives?

One thing that's true: *Temptations of the Flesh* are going to be here until the Lord comes. They are going to be here in the ways of our daily comings and goings, in the ways of our emotions, in the ways of our thinking--and, as I have experienced, standing in the way of God's blessings.

Not one person is worth trading for the blessings God has promised you. If I hadn't stepped aside when I did I would not have seen God's blessings unfold the way they did for me: a TV and a radio commercial, a major pharmaceutical contract, major speaking engagements flowed abundantly.

All this allowed me to see that when I denied the flesh and made God the priority, He granted me rewards for simply being obedient.

We have to learn to walk away from *Temptations of the Flesh*.

When or if I fall, I try never to fall in the same place twice. Instead of listening to music that's going to tempt my flesh, I let myself be serenaded with the sounds of the Gospel which is so beneficial to my spirit. For when you feed a part of you that is hungry the most, it asks for more.

More of Him is what I desire!

Temptations of the Flesh
How do we live without them?
We don't.

Coming soon:

Author DeVondia Roseborough will share Truth through the journeys of Regina BoRose, her friends, her so called friends, as well as other characters introduced in this novel along with new ones.

Regina will continue in three more adventures from the **Baptized N' Warm Milk Collection based on** *Temptations of the Flesh.*

About the Author

DeVondia R. Roseborough loves reading writing and empowering individuals who are lost inwardly and camouflaging outward. DeVondia is an inspiring motivational speaker, helping women and girls define their self-worth, Founder/President of The Rasberrirose Foundation Inc. This inspirational author writes solely on "True Life" experiences. DeVondia resides in Charlotte North Carolina with her two daughters and dog named "Butta"

To purchase books by DeVondia R. Roseborough or book her for your next event:

Email: Rasberrirose@aol.com
Web site: www.devondiaroseborough.com